THE WARRING HEART

Ros Rendle

SAPERE
BOOKS

THE WARRING HEART

Published by Sapere Books.

20 Windermere Drive, Leeds, England, LS17 7UZ,
United Kingdom

saperebooks.com

ISBN: 978-1-80055-375-0

ACKNOWLEDGEMENTS

Thanks to Scott Rendle for finding me the War Diaries from Kew Archives Offices for the relevant regiments and time frames. I was able to use these for research and accuracy.

My thanks also go to my mother, who was an author, and gave me the idea for this story. Her name was Christine Ellis.

The team at Sapere Books have continued to be helpful and supportive throughout the process of producing this book and I'm so grateful for their patience, skill, and knowledge.

CHAPTER 1

Pretoria Redfern looked at herself in the long cheval mirror. This, her first proper ball gown, shimmered as she moved. The Belle Époque was at an end and the news was on everyone's lips: war was finally declared after months of speculation. June 28th, 1914 caused the chain reaction, but it was the final event following many years of unrest that acted as the spark. The Archduke Franz Ferdinand, heir to one of the most powerful dynasties in the world, had been assassinated during his visit to the city of Sarajevo in Bosnia.

Papa had said they could still attend the ball after he had contemplated the situation, but he insisted their gowns should be loyal to the country.

Thus, although Pretoria's was made in Madame Sylvie's little emporium in the town, she was told to base it on a design by the House of Charles Worth. Although the couturier's son, Jean Philippe, was as French as they come, the father had been born in Lincolnshire, so there was a shred of patriotism. She would say to any who might ask that it was a Worth dress. The layers of soft blue fabric fell to Pretoria's ankles like a summer waterfall reflecting the sky, and ruffles of white cobweb lace were silvered with rhinestones around the hem of each tier. Although styles were veering towards more shapeless and austere designs, Pretoria's gown was cinched in at the waist. The sleeves were not too ornate, but still had a romantic outline in their soft gathered fullness. She was floating among the heavens as she swayed and turned to survey the rear. While the lace modestly covered the cleave between her young breasts, the back plunged daringly in a V. The bow at her waistline was another fall of water-coloured fabric.

Never had she had such a beautiful dress, and she was thrilled her father had allowed her to wear it to the ball tomorrow. It must have cost him a fortune, but perhaps Madame Sylvie had given him a bargain because Mr Redfern put so much business her way from his department store. Still, the harassed seamstress had stitched the frill at the neck upside down and Elise had been obliged to rectify it. Pretoria's thoughts were whirling. All was perfect, and surely this would encourage Simon to make his move and speak to her father.

"Shall I unbutton it now?" Elise, who had been with the family for more years than a donkey might live, stood waiting to help her young charge climb out of the confection. Her name was really Eliza Ann Ollerenshaw, and she was a raw-boned country woman from over the Pennine Hills in Yorkshire, but Mama had taken to Frenchifying everything, and even more so since the store had gained its Summer Court tearoom and enlarged the ladies' costumier department. Eliza had become Elise before Pretoria was born.

"Do you think I'll catch someone's eye tomorrow? I can't wait to make that entrance." Pretoria clapped her hands. "Surely Mr Simon Rashbrooke will be there."

"The colour certainly reflects the sparkle in those eyes of yours, Preti. I don't see how you can fail to gain attention. Just be a little demure for a change. You don't want to court gossip," Elise said. "You're not a hoyden, now. No more running about across the hills and messing about in the yard with a stick in the puddles."

"Don't look at me like that, Elise. I know what you are thinking."

The older woman regarded the glittering girl, and Pretoria recognised her maid's fondness. Many times, she had patched a torn dress or wiped a grazed knee when her own parents had been tied up at Redfern's Department Store, building the business that afforded the family their current luxuries. Elise had done her best to tame this wild child as she ran through the house and out across the lawn or jumped down the last three stairs instead of walking demurely. Pretoria understood the sigh that Elise gave. Those youthful times were passing, but the future looked rosy.

"Let's hurry now. Look at the time! I'm expecting Mr Rashbrooke at any minute. What would he say to see me in my undergarments like a Jezebel?"

"Miss Pretoria! Mind what you say, please. Come and sit and I shall tidy your hair. Look, I could wind these ribbons in, and they would match your dress."

"Dear Elise. What would I ever do without you? Thank you."

Once she was dressed for her afternoon walk in the park with Simon, she looked at herself in the mirror again and then at Elise.

"Yes, you do," Elise said with a grin.

"What?" Pretoria asked innocently.

"You look as fetching as any I've seen. Now go on with you and enjoy your walk."

Over the past couple of months, Pretoria and Simon had met at the quaint little hot chocolate shop in town. They had ridden across the moors and even galloped across the fields. Then there was that special evening recently; she remembered the tender, teasing smile that had lit his eyes as he'd smiled at her over the lid of her piano only last week.

"Miss Preti, you sing as sweetly as a thrush," he'd said. There was a tiny trace of West Country in his accent. "I may have the supper dance at the ball next week, may I not?"

As they entered the park on this warm August day, the sun was shining brightly, matching the rosy glow inside Pretoria. She hung on Simon's arm, looked up at him, and smiled.

"You look as pretty as any of these roses. Pink suits you, and the ribbons in your hair are the crowning glory," he said. Then he bent to pluck a bloom from the flower bed beside the path upon which they strolled. "It does not match your style and beauty, but it's all I have to offer you." He presented it with a flourish and a cheeky grin.

"Hey!" shouted the park keeper.

Simon took her hand and they scurried away towards the lake, where they threw themselves down on a bench and convulsed with laughter. After they'd caught their breath, Simon stood and offered Pretoria his hand. He pulled her to her feet so sharply she stumbled into him, which was his intention, she discerned.

"Mr Rashbrooke," she said primly, but couldn't hide a giggle as he apologised profusely.

"I hope you're not hurt," he said, a dimple appearing next to his mouth. "I might have to kiss you better." Casting a quick glance over his shoulder, he gave her the quickest of kisses on her cheek.

"Simon! What will people say? Behave."

He pretended to look contrite, and took her hand through his arm. They continued their stroll. They passed Mrs Parks with a young companion. Mr Moore was there too, sitting on a bench and looking serious. Mrs Strong passed with Rose and Izzy, although there was no sign of their sister Delphi, for which Pretoria was grateful. She had an inkling Simon would be distracted, as most other young men seemed to be when she was around. They nodded as they passed these various acquaintances, and Simon touched his hat. Pretoria was pleased hers had a wide brim, partly shielding her from curious glances. Though she pretended to be unaffected by what others might think, she couldn't help enjoying the envy on the faces of some. Simon must have noticed, for he leaned down and whispered in her ear, "You have a little smile like a kitty that stole some confectionery. What are you thinking?"

"Nothing to do with you," she said, laughing gently.

The following day, Pretoria was in an excited frenzy at the thought of attending her first formal occasion. Elise had said she wasn't sure that Mr Simon Rashbrooke was the right man to tame her, but they had been seeing much of each other lately. Pretoria's thoughts ran on. She had steadfastly ignored the rumours of his gambling and the suggestion of debts. That was more than likely the green eye of envy from others who would love to have the attentions she was enjoying, or perhaps it originated from some of the matrons who were peeved he had not chosen to court their daughters.

Oh, she would surely die of anticipation! It was a whole three hours to wait for her first major ball in town. Alright, so it wasn't Manchester, but it was just as grand in the rooms of the small spa town.

Having recently turned nineteen, Pretoria was positive she was ready for more out of life than being stuck at home with only the department store ahead of her, even if it was the largest one around. Times were changing, and her father persisted in encouraging her participation in the business. Curse her brother Michael for making it clear he was more interested in teacher training at Peterborough than taking over from Papa! That Emily Wilding Davison woman had died for the cause of women, but she wasn't yet sure it was her cause. She had no intention of being tied to the store. She was destined to become the wife of someone as dashing as Simon Rashbrooke, surely. Let her sister Tamsin take over. She had the brain as well as the work ethic. In four years, she would be Pretoria's age and more than capable of organising the staff and overseeing the books. She had a head for figures already.

Pretoria's parents had supported their daughters' education, and their upbringing had been forward-thinking. Pretoria read all manner of modern books, and had recently finished a new novel by Edgar Rice Burroughs borrowed from her brother, about a boy raised by apes. It was fairly shocking, but tremendous fun, and romantic in its way. She would have liked to live among the trees, swinging and free.

Her world was expanding. Romance was her craving. Surely tomorrow Simon would declare himself to her and then her father.

CHAPTER 2

The atmosphere was buzzing as Pretoria entered the great ballroom with her brother, Michael. He was home from his new recruits' training camp in Manchester, which was perfect. There were no uniforms available for them yet. That was a shame, but he wore the normal evening attire, and it suited his lean frame. He was tall and good-looking, with the same fair hair as her own. Elise had dressed hers with ribbons and pearls, which complemented her dress. She was confident they looked a fine pair as she entered on his arm, but she had to admit she was a little nervous. Her mother and father preceded them. Mr Redfern's white waistcoat stretched over his generous figure, but the black tailcoat disguised the fact to a degree. Pretoria watched as his whiskered countenance turned first one way and then another as he grinned at all he saw in his usual fulsome manner. Then he turned to his children, and gave a wink and a nod before muttering, "Grand, eh?" His wife sailed on his arm in her purple bombazine and lilac beaded net, like a ship in full sail, and nodded graciously to those of her acquaintance. The ostrich feathers in her hair bobbed in unison.

Mr and Mrs Strong and their two older daughters, Rose and Delphinium, who everyone called Delphi, were already there. The youngest sister, Iris, or Izzy was too young to attend such an event, as was her own sister, Tamsin. Pretoria saw Michael searching the room and guessed it was for the two Strong sisters. The Strong family were neighbours and the children had all grown up together, played together, and been schooled together. She knew Michael, like everyone, was drawn to

Delphi's beauty and elegance, although she had a sneaking feeling it was Rose whose eyes would follow Michael around the room.

Oh, where was Simon? He was taller than most, so she thought she would spot him easily as she waited her turn to descend the few steps into the throng. There was a buzz around the room as she stood looking, which seemed to grow louder. Were people gazing at and muttering about her? She preened and congratulated herself on her appearance. Then she mentally gave herself a good talking-to. How awful to be so conceited. No, she wouldn't be that. It was not attractive at all, not one little bit, so she lowered her eyes and determined to be more ladylike. It wasn't long before she raised her eyes to scan the room again, though. Surely Simon would come soon and ask her to dance. After all, he had made a point of reserving the supper dance with her. At the foot of the stairs stood Mr Nathaniel Moore. He nodded and smiled at her as she descended.

"Miss Redfern," he said, looking at her with a sardonic expression.

I don't know what he has to be derisive about, she thought. *Is he laughing at me? How dare he, and why? Do I have something out of place?* Her hand went to her hair in a sudden wave of uncharacteristic self-consciousness. *He doesn't matter anyway. He's as old as the hills.*

Pretoria was quickly distracted. The room was stunning in its modernity. Gone were the benches along the edges, for the wallflowers to sit and wait in the hope of being asked to dance. Tables and chairs were arranged for small groups with pristine white cloths. Beautiful posies of flowers in cut glass vases, which sparkled in the lamplight, sat in the centre of each. The huge marble fireplace was unlit, but a beaten copper plate in a wooden frame had been polished and burnished to reflect all the colours of the ladies' dresses, and there were fresh flowers on the mantel above. The wall sconces held electric bulbs, where candles would have been, as did the two massive chandeliers that were suspended from ornate white plaster roses on the ceiling.

The small music ensemble was placed on the dais at one end of the room. Pretoria was amused to see one of the women playing a large cello with tremendous vigour, while a tall, stringy, superior-looking man swayed as he bowed the strings on his violin. Then her attention darted away as she followed her parents around the edge of the dancefloor towards their allotted table. Waves of perfume assailed her nostrils. Chatter rose and fell, but only odd snippets reached her. Two or three times she got the sense that she was the topic of conversation before silence reigned as she passed. She nodded greetings to people, as she had seen her mother do. It must have been her imagination. After all, this was her first ball and she was probably a little oversensitive.

Michael pulled out the chair at their table, and Pretoria tried to look elegant, ensuring her dress was smooth as she sat down. It would be so embarrassing if, when she stood again, it was crumpled and ugly. Nor did she want to sit on the tails of the bow and pull it undone. Ah, this was so much more complicated than running over the hills in her everyday dress.

The musical quartet were playing something lively, and several couples were dancing already as Pretoria watched with anticipation. Her little slippers tapped the rhythm and her fan beat gently under the table. Then she quickly remembered it was bad manners in polite society to hide her hands and rested them on the table. Or was it only one hand that should remain in sight? *Oh, ridiculous*, she thought. The music echoed deep inside her stomach with her eagerness to be in the arms of her love. It was making her tense.

Michael was talking of the present situation in Europe with a friend who came across to greet him. Pretoria couldn't help but overhear.

"It's inevitable that trouble would follow his assassination," the other fellow said.

Pretoria gathered they were referring to the Archduke Franz Ferdinand. It was on the lips of everyone because of the powerful Austria-Hungary Empire, with all their complex alliances and enemy structures, which had led to this recent declaration of war. It was affecting all of them already. Pretoria was irritated. There was so much disruption and change on the horizon, but only for others. All the young men were excited, of course, and many, like her brother, had joined up regardless of parental wishes, yet she was stuck in the same place. *Life is unfair for women*, she thought.

"Why on earth they continued with their parade in that open-topped car after a bomb was thrown, is beyond me. Sophie the Duchess's face was grazed. Did you hear that? But twenty or more were killed and they made light of it." His expression was shocked.

"They did change their plans, though, to go and visit the wounded in hospital, and they say extra security measures were put in place," Michael said. "Didn't do much good though, did it? The way I heard it, the car went in the wrong direction and was turning right near where the bomb was thrown, which meant it was travelling exceedingly slowly. Ideal opportunity for the wretches to have another go. With the old emperor so ill, it's inevitable this would cause chaos. It's all history now, though, isn't it?"

His friend persisted. "Security was tighter four years ago for the emperor's visit than it was in June for this nephew of his. Ridiculous."

"Bosnia was always going to be a tinderbox, since Austria-Hungary annexed it."

"And now, all hell will be let loose, you see if I'm right." The friend nodded sagely.

"Things have moved fast. It'll be a grand adventure for us as a result." Michael rubbed his hands with glee.

"Enough, now, you two," Marie Redfern said. "Can we not forget all this upset for one night?"

"Yes, Mama."

"Sorry, ma'am. I do hope you enjoy your evening."

She nodded graciously.

The two exchanged a look and moved away, probably to continue their discussion elsewhere.

Throughout this exchange, while still listening, Pretoria had been scanning the room, but still there was no sign of Simon.

CHAPTER 3

Upon arrival, Mr Nathaniel Moore's eyes had raked the throng. It was already crowded with butterfly colours and the excited, chaotic whir of many voices rose to greet him. He nodded across people's heads at Mr Strong and noted how pretty Rose looked. Delphi was her usual magnificent self, already surrounded by several young men. Of course, their sister, Izzy, was younger than Tamsin Redfern, so she would be at home. He had heard how they liked to get into mischief together, so it was just as well they were excluded from a gathering such as this. Still, he liked Tamsin's spirit. He smiled at the thought.

Now he stood with carefully acquired, deceptively apparent ease at the foot of the steps. Only outwardly calm, his head turned with each new arrival. He was beginning to regret coming. So much for his brave words to himself about getting out into society again, rather than hiding himself away among his fields of wheat and barley, and his cows. After all, it was a good year and a half since he'd been jilted by Julia Worthington. She had turned out to be decidedly unworthy-*ington*. Huh! He grimaced to himself. He had survived — just.

Each time the double doors opened behind him, his breath quickened, and each time his heart stilled with disappointment. Nathaniel William Moore was on the verge of leaving and forfeiting the price of his ticket. Perhaps he'd give it another five minutes, but that was all.

Finally, the Redferns arrived, and there she was. Pretoria hung on her brother's arm behind her mother, who was with his friend of old, Benjamin Redfern. With the benefit of his thirty-one years, he could discern that Pretoria clung just a little too tightly. Was she nervous? Now there was a turn-up. From the foot of the short staircase, he caught the radiance of her youthful excitement. Even through his shortness of breath and the sound of the racing blood in his ears, he was aware of the quiet that descended as the family entered. He wondered if they had heard the ghastly rumours. Looking at Pretoria, he doubted it. Her eyes were roving over the crowded room, and he guessed straight away who she was looking for.

All summer he had watched and heard of her antics with the wretched Simon Rashbrooke. With hard-won patience, he had quelled his own longings. She was young and needed this experience. He would wait. He must hold back. He must linger and watch from the outside until she was ready, until she had sowed those wild oats; the seeds of the *Avena fatua*, so difficult to separate from the useful cereal crop and so persistent. As a land-owning farmer, he knew how relentless and tenacious they could be. It was a risky strategy, but it sounded like it might have been the right one, from what was transpiring on the gossip circuit. He hoped above all else that nothing would happen to her before the bounder was exposed.

Pretoria descended the few steps and he turned as she arrived by his side. "Miss Redfern." He greeted her with his warmest smile, trying desperately to convey his emotions without scaring her. She nodded and her eyes moved on with haste. He watched as Pretoria's slim figure swayed away through the crowds. Conversation halted around her, and his heart urged him to protect her from the hurt and humiliation that he was sure would come.

He gave it five minutes, almost counting each second in his head. Her brother was engaged in conversation with another fellow, but he barely noticed as he watched her roving eyes. Finally, he approached the table at which she sat with her parents. Her initial upward glance followed by a scud of disappointment across her face told him all he needed to know, but she was too polite to refuse him a dance. She stood and rested her fingers gently against his own and they moved to the dancefloor. Heat rose around his neck under the tight collar of his shirt as her skin seared against his. The quartet on the little stage played a waltz. It was perfect. As she rested her left hand on his shoulder and took his hand in her right, he placed his arm around her. As lightly as he could, he rested his fingers above her slim waist and below her left shoulder blade. He was aware of each muscle, each sinew, each breath that she took. Her body swayed close to his, and her perfume filled his senses. He searched for something entertaining to say, but he was never good at small talk, and especially not when there was so much he was desperate to whisper in her ear.

He knew the music would end very soon, so he plucked up his courage and said, "Perhaps I might have another dance later? Maybe the supper dance?"

"Oh, I think I am promised to someone else for that," she said.

Of course she was. How foolish of him. He knew that would be the case, but he had to ask anyway. His throat closed.

After a breath, he opened his mouth to speak when the whole room went silent, just for a moment, before conversation resumed at an even greater pace. Nathaniel turned. Pretoria tensed under his touch, and she gasped.

There was Simon at the top of the steps. How dare he come? Surely, he must know his presence would be unwelcome. Had all those rumours surrounding him reached the ears of this dear girl in his arms? Perhaps not.

The music drew to a close. Nathaniel hardly heard it, but all the movement around him stopped and Pretoria came to a halt too. He looked down at her in confusion and realised his moment of euphoria had come to an end. He led her back to her family with reluctance, thanked her and retired to his former position, resting one hand on the balustrade to steady himself.

A neighbour approached. It was Benjamin Redfern, his dear love's father. What might he want? Nathaniel's spirits rose. Perhaps he would give information on the condemnation of that damned fellow who had dared to show his face. "Good evening, Moore."

"Ah, Benjamin. Your daughter looks lovely this evening. How are you and Mrs Redfern?" Politeness satisfied, he took two deep breaths.

"This political situation is damned worrying, with that assassination in Sarajevo," Benjamin Redfern said, and Nathaniel's mood plummeted again.

"Yes, indeed."

"Why the Archduke and his wife had to go visiting on St Vitus day, I don't know. Seems like direct provocation to the Serbs, if you ask me."

Nathaniel frowned. "Sorry?"

"Well, I mean, that's their feast day if you like, eh? It's a national day of commemoration for the Bosnian Serbs, the day Austria-Hungary annexed that large chunk of their territory and some anniversary or other of a great defeat back in the day. They were never going to be happy to see him in Sarajevo and certainly not on that day, don't you see?"

"Quite." Nathaniel looked around. He was desperate to see if Pretoria was dancing or talking with Simon Rashbrooke.

"Well, Germany won't be too happy. The Kaiser and Franz Ferdinand were good friends."

Nathaniel dragged his attention back to the conversation. "Yes, absolutely. Germany has been sabre-rattling recently with the build-up of their navy, but hopefully it'll just be another local fracas in the Balkans. Best to get it over with sooner rather than later, I suppose." His eyes drifted past his friend's left shoulder to the dancefloor.

"I expect you're right. Hmm," Benjamin Redfern said. "I can't see Russia being too keen to get involved, though, eh? They're supposed to be an ally of Serbia, so it may be impossible to stay out of it."

"Yes, the Tzar's grandfather was assassinated, I think, so I suppose there's a sympathy between them. I say, do excuse me, good man, there's something…" Nathaniel escaped and made haste across the floor as if with a genuine purpose.

Pretoria was in the process of being whirled around the dancefloor by that libertine Rashbrooke. Had he no shame? Still, perhaps the rumours were untrue. Surely he would not show his face here in polite society if they were. Nathaniel stared. Pretoria's head was thrown back as she laughed and her blue dress whirled out as she spun, like the crest of a wave. Rashbrooke's hand was on her tiny waist. Nathaniel turned to go and find a drink. He couldn't watch this.

Halfway through the evening he decided he must have some fresh air. He left his glass on a table and headed out to the terrace. His head was light. On finally returning to the damp warmth of the room, he saw that it was the last dance before supper. Everyone was pairing off and heading to the supper hall. Still there was no sign of Pretoria. Or Simon, for that matter. He hadn't seen them outside, but perhaps he had missed them. Oh Lord! He hoped she hadn't done anything to put her reputation in jeopardy. Society might be changing, but not that much. No, please God, no. It would be so like her to care less, and risk all.

He rushed outside again, the drink giving him courage. He found her alone, leaning on the wooden railings around the edge of the terrace. Thank goodness. He was about to turn, when he realised she was crying. *If that bastard has done anything…* he thought. He hesitated. Perhaps she would prefer to be left alone.

I hope she's not hurt. With that, he advanced slowly and quietly.

She seemed agitated when she heard his footfall at last.

"I'm sorry," he said. "Is there anything I might do?"

"No, no. I'm fine."

"You clearly are not." He smiled at her with gentleness. He yearned to enfold and comfort her.

"Please! Leave me alone." Pretoria turned her head away.

"At least take this." He handed her his pristine white handkerchief.

She sniffed loudly in a very unladylike way, then giggled mirthlessly. "Excuse me," she said, before blowing loudly into the linen.

"You better keep that, now." He smiled at her again. "Would you like some supper?"

"No. Thank you for asking, though. I'll just stay here for a while. Please excuse me." She turned away from him and he withdrew with great reluctance.

CHAPTER 4

"Your father wants to see you in his study at eleven o'clock." Elise had pulled back the curtains and bright sunlight flooded the bedroom.

Pretoria screwed up her face and groaned. Now what had she done? Then memories of the evening before swamped her, and she turned her face to the pillow so that Elise would not see her tears.

They had been on the terrace. Simon had asked her to take some fresh air with him. Surely this was the moment. Her heart began to race as he took her hand and drew her outside. There were other couples, so all was quite alright. He'd made no attempt to encourage her to descend the steps to the lawn, which might have been a bit too much, although she would have been tempted to descend into the shadows with him. He rose even more in her estimation, should that have been possible, because he did not suggest it. He gestured to the far corner, away from the other people. Some eyes followed them, but Pretoria merely smiled, nodded and was secretly gleeful.

"The thing is…" Simon started.

Pretoria could hardly breathe. "Yes?" She leaned towards him.

"Well, I have to go away."

"Pardon?" This wasn't right.

"Yes. I must leave. In fact, this very night. I only came here this evening to tell you."

"But what about the supper dance?" Pretoria was confused. She started to prattle. "You asked me to save it for you. You're going away tonight?" she repeated.

"Yes. Now."

"Shall I see you next weekend?"

"No. I shan't return."

"But … I don't understand."

"We've had some fun. I like you a lot, but now I must go." His words were stark and his voice devoid of emotion.

"Go where? What do you mean?" Pretoria was aware of a slice of panic. This was not how it was supposed to be tonight. This evening he was going to ask for her hand, she was sure. What was he talking about?

Elise's voice brought her back to the present. "You better look lively, lass. It's already late. You mustn't keep your papa waiting. Look, I've put out a morning dress and I'll go and make you a cup of hot chocolate."

"Whatever can he want?" Elise seemed to be avoiding meeting her eager look, moving around the room to put out Pretoria's undergarments. "Elise! What does he want, do you think?"

"I'm sure I don't know." Her eyes slid away again. "You best be quick."

Perhaps Simon Rashbrooke had thought again. Perhaps he had been to see Papa after all, so that they could be married in haste, and she could go away with him. Her heart gave a skip. Yes, that could be it. Papa wanted to know if she was happy at the prospect of becoming Mrs Simon Rashbrooke. Oh yes, absolutely yes!

She ran down the stairs, jumping the last two and using the balustrade to give her momentum for the turn at the bottom, as she'd done in her youth. The heavy hem of her dress whirled out. She was filled with excitement and nervous apprehension.

Her papa turned from the window as she knocked and entered his study. He looked most serious as he stood with his hands clasped behind his back under his jacket, but he didn't look angry. "Ah, Pretoria, my dear. Come and sit. There, beside your mother, child."

Mama was not the most motherly of people but now she cleared her throat, patted the cushion next to her, and said in a quivering tone, "Come here to me, my dearest daughter."

Pretoria blinked at the strangeness of it all and crossed the room to join her mother on the edge of the unforgiving leather Chesterfield sofa. Mama didn't look pleased, as Pretoria had hoped. "Mama, what is wrong? You sound so distressed."

"I am. Decidedly so. *Très distrait*. Your father has some very disturbing news to share with you."

Papa became irritable. "Marie, for goodness' sake. Stop Frenchifying everything. Now is not the moment."

Pretoria experienced a jerk of fright and again she thought of Simon. Had he spoken to Papa, or had he indeed gone? What if Simon had suffered a terrible accident, or maybe one of her family? But no, for such a family upset her sister Tamsin would have been summoned, too. "Mama, what is it?"

Mr Redfern seated himself opposite them and cleared his throat. "It concerns a matter of the gravest importance." He nodded at her mama. "Your mother tells me it may cause you some distress, Pretoria."

"But what is it?"

"It's in relation to an acquaintance — someone, I regret to say, we had begun to count on as a friend."

"*Papa?*" Pretoria strove to keep exasperation from her tone.

"You must be brave, my love," Mama said in a sepulchral voice. "Summon pride to your side."

"It has come to my ears," said her father, "that your friend Mr Simon Rashbrooke has deceived us all."

Dizziness wrapped itself around the girl. *So, he has gone and now I may find out why. Surely there must be some explanation.*

Last night he had led her to believe he did not care and had simply decided to move on. The voice of her father receded. Both her parents began to disappear in a mist.

"Benjamin," Mama said with some force, "I think our girl is about to fai—"

Papa reappeared with alarming abruptness as he leaned forwards and peered at Pretoria. "My girl, are you alright? You've gone very pale."

"Put your head down." Mama put her hand behind Pretoria's head and made to push it lower.

Pretoria shook her off. "Sim— Mr Rashbrooke?"

"It is so disgraceful! Shocking! To have hoodwinked us all so callously." Mrs Redfern began to wring her hands.

"He abused our hospitality," Papa thundered. He was in his stride now. "He's entirely misled every one of us, all our friends too. One expects some integrity, honesty. Flirting outrageously with you all spring and half this summer. Paying you such obvious attention."

"Pursuing you openly until everyone must be expecting an engagement," wailed her mama.

"What has he done?" Pretoria raised both arms. "Tell me!"

"My poor child; prepare yourself." There was an interminable pause as Papa drew breath. "Mr Rashbrooke is already married but living apart from his wife. It might be 1914 and the world is indeed changing, but this is disgraceful behaviour."

Pretoria thought she might be sick. "Is it true? How do you know? It can't be so."

"There can be no possible doubt. I have spent the morning making enquiries. I went to the store and telephoned several people in the area from which he hails."

"How did you first hear?" Pretoria's voice was harsh and cracked.

"It seems it's the talk of the town. I heard something of it last night after he had left the ball. Thank goodness he took no liberties with you," Papa said.

"He didn't, did he?" Her mother cut in, clutching her hand to her ample bosom.

"The word is he has a child, too, though its whereabouts is a mystery. With the mother, one presumes."

"A child! Oh, how will I live this down?" Pretoria was mortified. "I must have been a laughing stock last night. I can't be seen out ever again." Tears flowed easily now as Pretoria thought back to the whispers that had followed her arrival at the ball. "I shall never be able to leave this house."

"You will, and hold up your face in the doing. Find another and do that quickly, then all will be forgotten," her mama said. "That's the best way to kill any more rumours and associations. Find another."

As Pretoria rushed from the room, all she could think about was the humiliation she must endure and that her life was over before it had even begun. The last thing she heard was her mama. "I'll send Elise to you."

Pretoria took the stairs two at a time, ran into her bedroom and flung the door shut with such force it must have shaken the house. She couldn't have cared less about that. She cast herself down onto the bed, clutched her pillow and wept in torrents.

When she had cried herself dry, she lay still, her face hidden in the crook of her arm, giving an occasional shuddering sigh.

She didn't move when someone quietly entered her bedroom. It would be Elise. Pretoria waited tensely, expecting to be told in brisk terms that there were more fish in the sea than ever were caught. Nothing happened, and presently a slight clicking made her turn her head a little. Elise was sitting on a chair by the bed, knitting. Knitting! When Pretoria's life lay in ruins.

"Elise, I … I think my heart is broken."

Next she would be told that hearts do not break at nineteen years of age, and that no man, no matter how charming, was a worthy cause for missing life. But Elise said gently, "And I dare say it is, Preti love, but hearts do mend. By gum, they have to. Yours may be badly bruised for a while, but 'twill mend."

"You cannot know how awful this is. How can you know that?" Pretoria demanded in a muffled voice. "All the time you have been here, you have never been in love."

"How can *you* be sure of that?" Elise answered.

There was a long pause. Pretoria rolled over and regarded her maid from under swollen lids. "Have you, then, Elise? Did you ever fall in love?"

"It may seem a strange notion to you, miss, but in fact I did indeed."

"Oh! Why have you never told us about it?" Pretoria sat up.

"Because it did not seem to me to be any of your business."

"Mmm." Pretoria paused for consideration. "No, I suppose not. I beg your pardon, Elise." After another silence, curiosity won. "Will you tell me now?" She blew her nose and scrubbed at her eyes.

Elise laid aside her knitting needles and wool. "I was younger than you are now. Just seventeen, but not too young to have feelings. He was a footman and the best-looking man I ever saw. And with most persuasive ways," she added after a pause.

"Elise! Did … did he make advances?"

"Aye, he did. I had just enough sense to check him."

"Did he want to marry you?"

"Marry me? Is it likely he would want to marry a gawk like me?" The maid scoffed but without trace of bitterness in her tone.

"What happened next?"

"What happened was that he put some other young girl in the family way and then eloped with yet a third, a parlour maid. I thought I'd ha' died of misery. Discovering one's idol to have clay feet is quite the hardest part to bear."

"Indeed, it is." Tears threatened to fall again, but Pretoria caught them in the sodden handkerchief she had balled in her palm. "I find it so hard to believe Mr Rashbrooke did not mean a single word of … of the compliments he paid me. I had imagined him to be so sincere."

"Perhaps he was," Elise said. She frowned and thought, before continuing. "Have pause to consider. Here is a young man of only twenty-two or twenty-three, was he? Bound for life to an older woman, as I hear it, and one who he cannot divorce by all accounts, her being a Catholic."

"How on earth do you know all this?"

"Oh, we hear stuff, in the kitchens." She continued. "He hopes to keep his youthful indiscretion a secret, perhaps, and then he meets you, a pretty young maid. Maybe he did fall in love at last. He knows there is no hope, but still he cannot drag himself from your company. Things drift along."

"So, do you think he might be true?" Pretoria was consoled by the notion and the romance of the idea.

"Could be. How can I say for sure?"

"Then … perhaps he may still find a way to communicate with me. In time, he might even be free himself."

"No, love, do not think along those lines for one moment." The well-known note of finality in Elise's voice sent the girl's heart plummeting into the toes of her pretty slippers. "Mr Rashbrooke will never be free unless in future years his wife dies, and even then, your father would never let you marry after this."

"I know he would not. Simon will never be welcome here or trusted ever again."

"So perhaps your mama is right in wishing you to hold up your head and face it out. I should not care a fig for spiteful gossip if I were you. It would not be like you to appear wilting after a young man has not played you fair."

"I had not thought of it in quite that light," Pretoria said.

"Then do so now. I'll be blunt. Everyone has been expecting a betrothal. They will all expect you to plead illness and back out of appearing at church in the morning or at the party next weekend. Inescapably, you would be an object of pity, even of some mockery. Do you wish for that?"

"No, of course I don't." Pretoria's back straightened.

"Then be brave and win the admiration of all."

Pretoria gave a shudder. "I shall try, and perhaps even Mama will be pleased with me."

"Good girl. Then get up and bathe your face. I shall set about heating the curling tongs and set you ready for the day. As I say, at church tomorrow face them all and be proud."

CHAPTER 5

As the Redfern family entered the church the next morning, Pretoria was vaguely aware of the scent of lingering incense mixed with the perfume of the orange lilies which adorned the arrangement at the base of the pulpit. Along with yellow alstroemeria and calendula in all their opulent glory, and some tall grasses, she concentrated on these so no one looking at her would have guessed at her inner turmoil.

Her new patriotic military-style coat, in dark green, with its modish epaulettes and double row of buttons gave her confidence. A charming little hat was perched on her head, and she held up her countenance with determined pride. She thought she noticed Delphi Strong whispering to her sister Rose, and Pretoria wondered if her expression was one of derision, but Rose frowned at her beautiful middle sister and shook her head gently, before nodding at Pretoria. Izzy, the youngest, sat with her mother, her German teacher Frau Schröder, and Frau Schröder's daughter, Gisela, who was about the same age. The two girls and Tamsin waved at each other, so perhaps they at least hadn't heard any ridicule.

As the Redfern family moved up the aisle to the empty pew they usually occupied, Pretoria noticed Mr Moore sitting on the end of his. He seemed to be watching her closely. It went some way to soothing her ruffled nerves to think he was admiring her, even if he was so much older. He was definitely too conservative to be of interest to her, but it was always pleasant to be noticed for a more flattering reason. At that, thoughts of Simon swarmed into her mind. The last time she'd seen him, he'd looked so tall and dashing and sadly remote.

She dug her thumbnail into her forefinger to quell any tears that might threaten to fall, smiled at Mr Moore, and moved on.

Nathaniel had turned each time someone came further down the aisle. All the farm workers that were left after the call-up and the serving classes tended to sit towards the back, allowing middle classes a place nearer to the alter. He had sat himself in the middle of the church but on the end of a pew, so he was in a prime position to see and greet those neighbours of interest to him. He prayed silently that Pretoria would not feign illness. If he knew anything of her, he guessed she would not, and he hoped she would dress in a brave armour and feign indifference to the small-town gossips. He had already heard them muttering.

As Nathaniel waited for the service to begin, his mind went over all he'd heard in recent weeks. In August, the Germans had invaded Belgium and north-east France, after years of sabre-rattling and increasing their forces. The Allies' retreat from Mons earlier in the month, with heavy losses, had been a disaster, and now the enemy was only thirty miles from Paris, which was concerning. However, the start of battle at the Marne had halted the Germans and Kitchener, God bless him, had secured support from the Fifth Army as well as the British Expeditionary Force. Sir John French was attacking the enemy forces and managing to halt their advance.

As he glanced around him yet again, Nathaniel's heart jumped, interrupting his thoughts. Pretoria Redfern was walking with her head held high. The peach-coloured fabric of her dress peeped from under her green coat as she strained to achieve an air of indifference with a slow, steady gait. His pulse raced a little faster, as every so often he glimpsed her slim ankles. He looked up hastily at her lovely face and was mesmerised by the sight of her looking so brave, as he'd hoped she would. That blaggard, Simon Rashbrooke, had much for which to answer.

As he focused on her, he was rewarded by a tight smile, and he guessed her nonchalance was hard-won. She passed on, and the family took their regular seat across the aisle from his own place. As such, he had a good view of her slim neck and her profile, and it was all he could do not to stare as she bowed her head in prayer after placing her little book on the ledge in front of her.

The rector arrived and they all stood. Following the opening welcome and short prayer, again Nathaniel could not drag his eyes away and watched as Pretoria smoothed her coat behind her as she sat.

Nathaniel listened with greater concentration as the rector spoke of their own boys who were away.

"Many of our own local lads have taken the call and gone to Manchester. Parents sat here before me can be proud and pleased that they are still training there, though biting to go overseas, probably. Still, it should all be over soon. They are holding their position well now, after the initial battle earlier in the month."

That's not quite how it's been, Nathaniel thought.

"Our brave soldiers have checked the German advance, put an end to their two-front strategy and their so-called Schlieffen Plan. I know, I know —" he held up his hands in surrender, which seemed highly inappropriate to Nathaniel — "they are entrenched on both sides currently, but remember this is the race for the sea, and our boys are keeping us safe here at home. Perhaps our own boys will be spared, as many say it will be over soon, possibly even by Christmas."

Nathaniel hoped so too, so he could continue as he was, on his land. He hadn't signed up with the others. People relied on him, but he had an itch of guilt about staying home. No one had given him a white feather. They knew in local circles that he was working on their behalf, and he was respected.

"Let us spare a thought for the new battles in the air, too." The rector's sombre voice rumbled on. "Who would have thought that a French aeroplane would fight a battle in the air with a machine gun? Such are the times of technical prowess in which we live. God bless the allies in this, our just cause. Let us pray."

At the end of the service the congregation filed out, and the rector shook hands and smiled at each person at the door. The Redfern family were already in conversation when Nathaniel exited into bright, crisp sunshine, which made him blink like a mole. He looked around and immediately spotted Pretoria. She was smiling and pretending to pay attention to a matron and her daughter. She nodded, but he could tell that she was not actively listening as her own mother glanced at her and spoke, probably on her behalf. He wanted to go and enfold her in gentle arms and sweep her troubles away, but he had to stand and watch.

As he glanced around, he saw several matrons and older men scowl at the German teacher employed by the Strong family for their youngest daughter, and he doubted she would be with them for much longer.

He saw young Tamsin with her friends Gisela and Izzy. They were whispering and probably plotting mischief. *It must be exceedingly difficult for the young German girl, currently. Many men of that nationality are being whipped off to imprisonment camps, in case they are spies. Some have been living in this area for years, and it seems unlikely that's what they are, but people are being so careful now, and quite judgemental*, he thought.

He stood nearby as Marie Redfern and Pretoria spoke with Mrs Margaret Parks and a young lady he did not know so well. He had seen her at some functions lately, although not at the ball last night.

"How charmingly that shade of green suits you, Miss Redfern. Almost like the pond in the town centre," the insufferable matron said. "Have you met my cousin by marriage, Miss Emily Parks?"

The ladies touched fingertips, as politeness demanded.

"A pleasure, Miss Redfern," the young newcomer said. "You look snug and patriotic. But tell me, where is that charming man, your customary esquire? That delicious fellow, Mr Simon Rashbrooke."

There was an appalled silence. Nathaniel thought the whole company had stopped chattering to look around or listen to the reply. Despite his observance of her desperate determination, he saw the tell-tale scarlet flood Pretoria's face, and tears glistened in her eyes, although she managed to stop them falling.

Margaret Parks tittered, before saying, "Emmy dearest, you have made a *faux pas*, but of course you could not have known. I only heard myself a few hours ago. Our handsome man is in direst disgrace."

"Miss Pretoria, I wonder if I might ask your opinion?"

Blindly clutching at any diversion, perhaps, Pretoria turned at the sound of her name. Nathaniel gazed down at her desperation. As she looked into his eyes, he smiled gently, her rescuer, he hoped.

CHAPTER 6

The Redfern family had known Nathaniel Moore for many years, but not well. The local society had been pleased when he had become engaged to Julia Worthington. She was a vivacious beauty with flashing eyes and dark red hair, one of the town's elite, and sought after by many bachelors of 'the set'. Quite a catch, they all said. Later, they had been subsequently shocked and, if truth be told, excited, when she had cast him aside almost on the eve of their wedding to run away with Lord Doddington. It was the talk of the town.

Nathaniel immediately left England for foreign climes and in the ensuing months, little had been seen or heard of him. Just over a year ago, shortly after his father's death, he had reappeared to take the inheritance of the farmhouse, its tenant properties, and all its lands. He and Mr Redfern had become reacquainted at some of the gentlemen's functions in the town, and they had all met at parties and gatherings over the past months.

Pretoria was grateful now as he led her away from the vile Mrs Parks. Looking up into his grey eyes, she said, "Thank you, Mr Moore. You saved me from an awful woman and her equally ghastly cousin." Her spirit would not be broken, of that she was determined.

"I could see, and hear, that it was an unnecessary conversation."

"Yes, well…"

Pretoria had almost ceased to notice Mr Moore's existence, yet here he was, her saviour from an odious situation. Quite the white knight. She'd always thought of him as being so much older than herself and her special group of friends; she still did. He seemed to be verging on dreary middle age, but it was kind of him to swoop in and rescue her.

"Nathaniel!" Mr Redfern came up behind them and took Nathaniel's hand. Pretoria excused herself and moved to greet Rose Strong, who was always gentle, kind and understanding.

"My dear Preti," Rose said, "what fun we had at the ball on Friday night, and it was lovely to see your brother again."

"Yes, he was only home for the night and had to return the next morning."

"So many young men have signed up to go to war, full of excitement, vigour, and misinformation, and we've been left, all us lasses and matrons, to worry and wonder what will become of them. Still, the thought of going overseas and having a grand adventure is enticing and those who had slight misgivings, like Michael, have been pulled along with the general fervour of others, I suppose."

"Yes, indeed, and now such social occasions as the ball will be curtailed, much to the chagrin of us who are still here," Pretoria said.

Rose looked sympathetic and nodded.

Over Sunday luncheon, Pretoria was quiet, moving her food around her plate.

"Not hungry, my dear?" Her mother surveyed her face.

"No."

"You need to eat, and Cook has gone to a lot of trouble with this roast beef. It's delicious, is it not, Mr Redfern?"

He harumphed in response as he tucked into a full forkful.

Pretoria looked at the meat and all the trimmings of roast potatoes, cabbage, carrots, and parsnips. She had a tiny taste of the latter before biting her lip and sighing again. The morning had been an ordeal, and now she was exhausted.

"This afternoon we shall go for a stroll in the park. That will freshen you and put the sparkle back in your eyes," Marie said. "You must get over this little setback. It is simply *un peu énervé*."

Pretoria resisted raising her eyes to the ceiling. *More than a little*, she thought. Her life was over. Could they not see that?

Tamsin touched her arm and gave her a smile of encouragement. She was a sweet child, still full of the joys of uncomplicated enthusiasms. Pretoria had watched her outside the church with that German girl, Gisela, and her usual partner in mischief, Izzy. They had been giggling and planning some scheme together. Pretoria wasn't interested anymore. At one time, she would have demanded to become involved.

"You need to find yourself another suitor, and fast," Papa said, before taking another mouthful of food. "Mm, this is good. Yes, another fella will take you out of yourself and stop all the idle chatter of empty-headed housewives." He glanced at his own wife and decided to say no more.

Pretoria knew full well he considered women to be uncomplicated creatures who could be jollied through a crisis with a new hat … or a new suitor.

She had to admit, the stroll through the park was pleasant. The sun shone brightly, although it wasn't strong enough at this time of year to warm the chilly breeze.

"Oh, look over there," Tamsin said. "It's Mr Moore. He's lovely. Quite good-looking, in an older kind of way, and so tragic after he was left alone following that awful Julia episode."

"How on earth do you know of that? You are just a child, Tamsin," Pretoria said. "As for tragedy, you know nothing. Stop prattling, *please*."

"I know he has a deep fancy for you." Tamsin pulled a face at her sister.

"I beg your pardon? Stop it! That's more rubbish."

"Girls, stop bickering. It's very unladylike," Mama cut in.

"Well, she called me childish," Tamsin said.

"No, I didn't, but I shall now. What you are saying is childish nonsense. He cannot possibly have the least interest in me. Anyway, he's old. You talk about things of which you know nothing."

"I do so. I saw him watching you after church this morning, and he drew you away from that awful Mrs Parks to spare you."

"Girls!" The warning in their mother's voice was clear.

Pretoria couldn't resist one parting shot. "I'm sure he has no interest in anyone since he was jilted. Everyone knows that."

It appeared that the path Mr Moore was taking would cross their own. "Hush now, or he'll hear what you say," Mama said.

Pretoria felt a gentle heat spreading around her neck and up to her ears, and wished fervently that it did not turn into a blush.

"Ladies, how lovely to meet you again," said Mr Moore, but his gaze was directed at Pretoria.

She was aware of Tamsin's smirk and narrowed her eyes at her sister before turning her gaze to Mr Moore. He was definitely not as good-looking as Simon, but he had a kindly face and pleasant grey eyes.

"I'm pleased to have bumped into you," Mr Moore continued. "Mrs Redfern, as you have your delightful younger daughter with you, might I borrow Miss Pretoria? There is something I would like to discuss with her. We shall only walk a while, and then I shall accompany her home, of course."

Pretoria was so startled she was unable to say anything. Her mother looked at her, and, seeing no reluctance, she agreed that it would be fine.

"Good afternoon, then, Mr Moore. We shall see you later." Before more could be said, Mrs Redfern hustled Tamsin away and Pretoria was left standing with Nathaniel.

"Shall we sit for a while?" Without waiting for her response, he walked across to a bench which overlooked the lake at the side of the path. Ducks squawked their mocking response as Pretoria toddled in his wake.

"I … I mustn't stay long," she said.

"A short time will suffice. Sit back and relax. You look exhausted. I imagine this morning was an ordeal. Close your eyes and listen to the sound of the fountain playing into the water. It's refreshing."

Pretoria did lean back, but she didn't close her eyes. The sun was warm on her face, and the droplets showering from the fountain glistened like crystal prisms. The patter into the lake was relaxing. The sound of laughter and voices softened by distance began to blur, and Pretoria's eyelids were becoming heavy as drowsiness enfolded her into a soothing melancholy.

Simon, where are you now? Did I really mean so little to you? she wondered, and she almost forgot about Nathaniel Moore's silent presence.

"I have a confession to make," Nathaniel said quietly, dragging her back to the moment. "I have something to ask you. Would you mind if I call on your father tomorrow and request that we might be married?"

Pretoria's eyes shot open, and she sat bolt upright. "Mr Moore…"

"Why Mr Moore?" he interrupted, gently mocking. "Our families have known each other for quite a while. Call me Nathaniel." Then he continued as if musing to himself. "I imagine this has surprised you, but you see I cannot afford to waste any more time. Tell me, is this your first proposal of marriage?"

"Yes," said Pretoria, too taken aback to be anything but truthful.

"Poor little one," he said, and Pretoria looked down as he lightly touched her arm with the tips of his long fingers. "It must be very disappointing for you," Nathaniel added, with only the merest hint of teasing in his voice. "I am certain you must think me too old, and I should be down upon one knee vowing my passionate and undying devotion to you."

"No, really, there is no need for that," Pretoria said, alarmed at the thought. She glanced around, hoping that no one she knew was close by. This was all highly embarrassing.

"I am glad you are prepared to release me from that obligation," he said in a perfectly solemn tone. "I feel sure it would be excessively uncomfortable. The dew must be rising by now, and I should probably get grass stains on the knees of my trousers. Besides, it might embarrass you, for I am sure that you are not in love with me at all."

To Pretoria's horror, tears began welling again. It must be because she was so tired. She bit her lip fiercely to control them, but two crept from under her lashes. Nathaniel smudged them away gently with his thumb, and she caught the subtle scent of something masculine but agreeable, which gave her a flutter deep down below her stomach.

"Don't weep, little one. Believe me, I, of all our acquaintances, understand how you are feeling, but it will pass. Are you interested in knowing why I should like to marry you?"

Pretoria nodded and gave an unladylike sniff. He had taken her so utterly by surprise. Was he serious, or playing some teasing game with her? She looked into his eyes and did not see him as a cruel man.

"There are a number of reasons." He leaned back and away from her. "Firstly, my mother has been pestering me to find a wife since I inherited my father's lands. In fact, she gives me no peace on the subject. I don't see her much, now she has moved away, but she writes often. She has her long-time companion with her."

Pretoria was not at all impressed with this reason. Was he tied to his mother's apron strings? She gave a small sigh, which he must have discerned, for she saw a smile tickle his mouth when she peeped up at him.

"I only see her infrequently, as I say, so you would not be troubled by a mother-in-law. She lives in Devon. She will not come visiting regularly to cramp how you manage things. Secondly," he continued, "I think you are an extremely beautiful girl who would fill the position charmingly."

"You make it sound like a job interview," Pretoria said, although she was partially mollified by his compliment.

"There are many kinds of love," Nathaniel said.

Pretoria flicked a quick look at him again and saw him looking across the water and off into the distance.

"The romantic kind may bring moments of delicious ecstasy, but it can also bring the bitterest pain and heartbreak." Then he muttered, "I should know."

Pretoria stayed silent.

More loudly, he added, "I should like to protect you from the gossips from whom you have so recently suffered."

Again, Pretoria stayed silent.

Nathaniel cleared his throat. "So, I come to my third reason. I should love to have an heir."

"I see," Pretoria said.

"Yes," said Nathaniel, "that will be part of the arrangement, but once it is accomplished, I will not trouble you further."

"We are making a business arrangement?"

"If you wish to see it as such, but I do hope it will be more than that in time."

"And what do I get from this arrangement?"

He paused. "Respect, an exceedingly good position in society as my wife, whatever you wish for in the comfort of our home, and all the other things that may bring, such as the protection I have already mentioned." Again, a small smile played on his face, which was not unpleasant. "Do not worry, I am not asking for a momentous decision right now. Merely that you will not object to my asking your father's permission to pay my serious addresses to you."

This weighty and old-fashioned little speech was amusing to Pretoria. Her embarrassment disappeared, but then she hung her head. "My life is all but over anyway, so I suppose I cannot object," she said.

"Good, that's settled, then. We will not speak of personal matters again for the moment. That can spoil a perfectly good afternoon walk in the park." Nathaniel stood. He offered Pretoria his hand, so she joined him. There was no pulling her towards him as Simon had done. There was no plucking of an illicit rose with which to present her, no cheeky smile and carefree laughter, but he tucked her hand in the crook of his elbow and gave it a reassuring pat as they proceeded to stroll towards the gates of the park. "Don't be afraid, my dearest," he said, and strangely she didn't feel scared at all.

All Pretoria wanted was to go home and let Elise tuck a blanket around her while she curled up on the settee in her bedroom before the coal fire.

"Shall I tell you of my travels abroad? Have you ever visited the south of France?" Nathaniel seemed perfectly at ease, while Pretoria was struggling to form any thoughts at all.

"No, I haven't," was all she could summon.

"As soon as this wretched war is done, maybe next spring, you may have the chance." He began to describe some of the places he had visited in Italy, Germany and the Netherlands, picking out the droll moments and poking fun at himself. Their walk home was soon done, and Nathaniel's parting shot was, "Until later." He turned and strode away. Pretoria stood in a daze and watched, before turning and opening the heavy door.

CHAPTER 7

Pretoria fell asleep in her cocoon on the settee. When Elise entered the room to pull the curtains across and bank up the fire, she blinked at the brightness of the modern electrical light fitting in the centre of the ceiling.

"You had better stir yourself quickly, Miss Pretoria. Your mama requires you downstairs and looking your best, as soon as possible. You better have a clean frock. That one looks decidedly creased, like a dishrag." Elise gave her a quizzical look. "Mr Moore is in the study with your papa and has been for the last half an hour."

"Oh!" Pretoria shot up, shedding the blanket. "My hair looks like I've been pulled through a hedge," she wailed as she glanced in the mirror.

"Did you know he was coming? I wondered if perhaps he had come to see Mr Redfern on a matter of business, although that would be unusual on a late Sunday afternoon. Then your mama asked for you."

Pretoria was ripping pins from her hair and reaching for her hairbrush.

"Here, give me that." Elise took the brush. "Let me straighten it out for you. We can't have you mussing it now, can we? Next you'll be mithering me that it's in a tangle."

Once Pretoria was re-clothed and her hair sorted out, Elise stood back and looked at her charge. "There. Pretty as a painting. 'Twill satisfy your mama and certainly convince the gentleman he has made a wise choice."

"What do you mean? I thought you said he'd come on business."

"Maybe, of sorts. What do I know?"

Pretoria's stomach turned with sudden anxiety.

"Get along with you downstairs, Preti, love," Elise said, "but mind you do not let your mama persuade you into something you really cannot bear to do. 'Tis not worth that. I'm always here for you."

"I know you are." Pretoria hugged the rotund little woman and hurried from the room.

As she traipsed down the stairs, withholding the leap at the bottom, she was not a little apprehensive and certainly unsure how to handle this situation. She could not bear all the talk and sniggering behind hands that she had experienced at the ball and again at church. *Was that only this morning?* she thought. *This might be a way out. Nathaniel Moore doesn't seem to want too much from me and is certainly comfortably well-off. Enough to hint of foreign travel when things allow.* She decided she better try to be demure and let things play out a little before deciding anything.

"Ah, there you are, Pretoria. Come and sit by your mother." Her father spoke, and her mother patted the seat, beaming at her.

"You will never guess," the matron said. "Mr Nathaniel Moore is in the drawing room. He has spoken at length to Papa. Is this the reason he wanted to walk with you earlier, by any chance?"

Mr Redfern cleared his throat with loud theatricality. "Pretoria, you see, after what transpired so recently, we must know your feelings. We cannot lend support to something which may seem totally abhorrent to you. Humph! You understand?" He took out a huge white handkerchief and needlessly wiped his face.

"We realise the news of Mr Rashbrooke's duplicity came as a shock, dearest," Mrs Redfern added, "but we are proud of the manner in which you overcame your distress and took our advice."

"Your advice?"

"To take heart and be pleased to encourage some other acceptable beau. Mr Moore is quite one of the wealthiest people in our area."

A wave of anger engulfed the girl. "I most certainly have not encouraged anyone. This is all a complete surprise to me…"

"Of course, my dear. *Calme-toi*. It's just that after all the upset and shame, this is the best possible outcome, is it not?"

Pretoria said nothing but was too exhausted and confused to do anything but acquiesce. "I suppose so."

"So, we may take it that you do not object to Mr Moore?" Papa asked jovially, his thumbs stuck in his waistcoat pockets.

"No, I do not object."

"Good, good," he said.

"Such a relief. He is a most charming man, and will make a perfect husband," Mama chimed in.

"But … but we are not betrothed." Pretoria spoke louder than she'd intended. "He has only asked permission to escort me, surely." A snake of panic crawled coldly around her neck.

"Certainly, dear child," Mrs Redfern said. "A reasonable time must elapse before you give him a definitive answer. Say, a month, but I'm sure we are all quite certain what the eventual outcome will be."

Pretoria was silent, confused all over again. It seemed to be more or less expected that she would marry Mr Moore, yet she hardly knew him. If she really could not have Simon, then she supposed that one day in the future she would have to marry someone, but this was happening so fast.

"Well, this is excellent. Nathaniel, as you may call him under the circumstances, is waiting in the drawing room. I suggest you go and invite him for luncheon tomorrow."

"Papa, I couldn't. You go and see him."

"I shall do no such thing."

"Go and be charming to him, Pretoria," Mama said, "and I shall ask Elise to bring a tray of sherry wine. You men may have whisky when we arrive."

Pretoria crossed the hall towards the drawing room. The sinking sun streamed across the floor and caught the dancing dust motes, but she took no pleasure in it, or the view of the gardens with the lingering chrysanthemums throwing a last burst of colour. Before she opened the door, she took a deep calming breath, determined to appear detached. Heaven forbid he would think her keen to marry for gain. She opened the door.

Nathaniel appeared not to have sensed her presence. He was standing to one side of the fireplace with his arm resting along the marble mantelpiece, gazing down into the flames, and she was several paces into the room before he moved his head. A wide smile lit his whole countenance which, in turn, surprised Pretoria into seeing something other than pure business.

"Ah, my dear Miss Redfern, Pretoria. Have you been speaking with your parents?"

"I have."

"With a happy outcome for me, I hope." His grey eyes were full of repressed mischief.

"Mr Moore. Nathaniel," she responded, "you are cordially invited for luncheon with the family tomorrow, and soon Mama and Papa will join us for an early evening aperitif."

"And who is doing the inviting? You or your mama?"

"Naturally, I second the invitation." Pretoria prayed he would pick up on her cool detachment.

"Then I cordially accept," he said. "Let us forget formality for a moment, mignonette, my Preti. I am sure it will be easier for us both if we are relaxed."

"You have no right to call me that," Pretoria said, managing to look superior, she hoped.

But all he did was chuckle. "You are right. I have not — yet — but it suits you so well."

"Mignonette means a slice of beef tenderloin." Pretoria looked puzzled.

Nathaniel threw back his head and laughed uproariously, and she watched as his Adam's apple bobbed. "That's mignon, and not the same thing at all."

She was thrown into utter confusion, and the advantage of superiority she had achieved disappeared in a puff.

"There is a mignonette flower, known as the little darling of blooms. It has the most fragrant perfume." He laughed again at her discomfort.

At that moment, the door opened, and Mama sailed in. Papa followed, and then Elise brought a tray of glasses and gave her a wink, so she was saved from further comment.

CHAPTER 8

Nathaniel Moore was reading the newspaper, with his breakfast tea at an easy distance to one side. Far from the war being over by Christmas, it was spreading and deepening. There was further unrest between the Serbian and the Austria-Hungarian forces. The British Indian army had clashed with Ottoman Empire forces near Basra in Iraq, and closer to home in Belgium there was a stalemate at a place called Ypres, where the Germans and Allies were both trying to secure the town. It was a strategic gateway to the coast, and also to valuable mineral mining sites. If the Germans gained the road to the French coast through here, it would be the end of Britain as they knew it. There were stories of trenches being dug, in which troops were living. They ran from Verdun on the Alsatian frontier round to the sea at Nieuwpoort and Dunkirk, a distance of more than two hundred and fifty miles.

Nathaniel took a distracted slurp of his tea and was troubled by what he read. On his farms he was working hard but living a comfortable life, and no real change had occurred to prevent this. His forthcoming marriage was on track, and he was content, apart from this news. There was the strong suspicion that the lull in the advance by the Germans at Ypres was only temporary while they re-grouped, rather than a cessation of attack. France was determined to wrest back their territories of Alsace and Lorraine lost before the war, and demanded support from their British Allies, so there would be no giving way at this place. The Germans already held the coast at Antwerp. Nathaniel could see they must be kept from Calais at all costs.

The Gordons and the Royal Scots, already plastered with dirt and their kilts heavy with winter rains, were waiting for the bombardment to finish so they could cross the battleground, he read. They were fighting in more than one direction to protect the salient created, as the horseshoe ridge around Ypres had been impenetrable and enemy fire rained down. It sounded awful and Nathaniel believed the newspaper was only telling half the story. He began to feel even more guilty sitting in the comfort of his warm farmhouse. He pictured soldiers from both sides lying where they had fallen in the oozing filth.

His work on the land was important to the war effort, too, he told himself. The country needed to eat, and his remaining workers needed direction from him, but his estate manager might have to do the managing without him if this continued much longer.

The wedding was decided for February. Marie was in a fluster to get everything ready. Part of her wanted to see her daughter safely wed and out of harm's way. The other wished to ensure all was ready for a fine show. She said as much, several times, to Pretoria, who simply wanted it over.

"You will enjoy your new home and it will fill your time, so you won't have to pine about what could never be. We are all better for that … that creature who deceived us so shamefully being gone. I heard from Mrs Parks that he has gone to war in France."

"Mama, I have no wish to hear," Pretoria said as she tried to stand still. The dressmaker had left the room to fetch some more pins, and Marie offered her opinion of Simon Rashbrooke in a hurried whisper. Suddenly, his desertion and this wedding became more real and inescapable. Pretoria lurched from excitement to fear.

Nathaniel suggested a honeymoon in York or Scarborough, but Pretoria was reluctant. She had no wish to bump into anyone she knew in the cathedral city when she was trying to learn how to become a wife, and the weather was not conducive to being by the sea. Nathaniel declared he was more than happy to show her his home as soon as possible.

As the day came closer, Pretoria found she was becoming waspish, and her younger sister bore the brunt. "Tamsin, you really are naughty," she said as she came upon her sister late one afternoon when the light was dimming in the drawing room. "You always have your nose in a book at forbidden hours. You will ruin your eyes, and what have you hidden in your skirt?"

Tamsin looked sullen. "Nothing but my pen. I was writing. I'm making a list, not reading. Look." She held up her pen.

"And ink on your fingers, honestly. A list of what?"

Tamsin compressed her lips. "Nothing," she said, and Pretoria thought she looked furtive, but then her little sister distracted her. "Don't be so smug," Tamsin said. "You think you are quite perfect now you have secured such an excellent marriage for yourself."

"What exactly do you mean by that?" Pretoria leaned forward and glared.

"Only a short while ago you were crying over Mr Rashbrooke. I should consider it unworthy to change *my* allegiance so swiftly."

"You spiteful little… You know nothing of the matter. Do not censure my behaviour." Pretoria took a step forwards, consumed by the desire to give her sister a box on the ears, but then a sneaking knowledge that her words might be true held her back. "I advise you to keep your clever nose out of things that do not concern you."

As the days wore on, Pretoria realised her engagement held certain advantages. It was not the romantic affair she had always imagined, but Nathaniel made the correct gestures. He sent her flowers and presented her with a gold bracelet, accompanied by a charming card. He did not recite poetry, and he did not pretend to be madly in love with her, much to her relief, but now and then he startled her into pleasure by some unexpected remark. He only called her mignonette, or Preti, on the rare occasions when they were alone. These were few in the weeks prior to the wedding as Marie whirled her daughter into more dress fittings, purchasing shoes and gloves and sorting out nightgowns and undergarments. For Pretoria, it was both exciting and exhausting and gave her less time for worrying.

However, at night she indulged in romantic dreams, and just before she slept she imagined Simon Rashbrooke reappearing to carry her off from under Nathaniel's nose. Sometimes she awoke with tears on her pillow and an agony of longing to see him. During the day, she reminded herself that if they were ever to meet again, she would treat him with icy disdain.

Nathaniel recommended himself to Pretoria in a surprising way. He knew just how to handle Mama. It was the day following her tiff with Tamsin when Marie called Pretoria to her side. Once she was bent on a project, Mama did not let things rest. "Pretoria, *chérie*, we must make lists."

"What lists, Mama?"

"For the final arrangements concerning your wedding, goose. For a start, have you chosen your attendant? I thought your friend Izzy. She's younger and so sweet. She likes fine clothes, but she's not as tall and pretty as you. It is essential that the whole bridal procession must present a charming picture."

"Surely it will be Tamsin?"

"No, no. She is too tall, and anyway she will not want to. She hates to dress up in finery. She's more interested in things at the store, finances and such. She's too much the tomboy."

"But Mama…"

"I have already spoken to her, and she says she does not want to."

Pretoria doubted this was Tamsin's genuine desire but said no more. Despite their differences, she loved Tamsin and did not wish her to be excluded if she was merely being manipulated into her decision. When Pretoria asked her sister, her worry was confirmed. Later, she confided in her betrothed.

At dinner that evening, Nathaniel was also present. He said, "It is fortunate that Pretoria has a sister who will be able to perform the duties of attendant to the bride. Tamsin, you must be so pleased to have the opportunity for that position." His innocent expression rested upon Marie.

Tamsin's face brightened.

"You are so wise and fortunate in your planning, Mrs Redfern, and we shall have a charming picture to present, shall we not?" Nathaniel smiled at her.

Pretoria saw her mother melt under his charming gaze and grinned inwardly.

CHAPTER 9

Pretoria awoke on the day of her wedding with mixed emotions. She had managed to push away thoughts of what marriage would mean, but this morning she could not forget Nathaniel's third reason for asking her to marry him. Unlike a couple of her friends, she knew how babies were made. She'd seen dogs in the stables at it, and when she'd questioned Elise when she was about fourteen, Elise had been honest with her. She hadn't liked the idea at all at that time, and the thought of her parents doing that mortified her. Thank goodness she had never had to discuss it all with her mama. She'd had time to get used to the thought since then, although she couldn't imagine herself doing that with a man.

Her mother and sister knocked on her door before bursting in. "Come on, lazybones," Tamsin said, "there is so much to prepare. At least the sun is shining. That must be a good omen after all the wind and rain we've had."

"As soon as we've breakfasted, we shall see to your hair and make-up. Come, come." Mama clapped her hands.

The minutes flew, and before she knew it, Pretoria was on her way, sitting with her papa in the carriage he had hired. The skirt of her cream silk dress hung in graceful folds, while the bodice was overlaid with Guipure lace and had a small stand-up collar. Mrs Redfern had ensured she had access to the finest of fabrics and had acquired a length of the new tulle for Pretoria's veil, which flowed to her hem and was held in place on her head by a circlet of hothouse flowers, acquired at huge expense at this time of year. They reflected those in the large bouquet she carried.

Tamsin and Izzy looked fetching in their pale primrose dresses as they stood waiting for her at the church door. Their wide-brimmed hats were trimmed with delicate yellow muslin and they each held a posy of white flowers.

As Pretoria walked down the aisle on her father's arm, she was tempted to shed some tears, but she managed to blink away any that threatened to fall, and she pasted on a smile. Nathaniel would be a kind and considerate husband, she was sure. When she looked up to see him ahead of her, he smiled gently, and she guessed he was aiming to reassure her.

His hair was neat and his suit emphasised his broad shoulders and long back as the sun slanted through the stained glass, casting a rosy glow over him. Perhaps this would not be so bad, and she would learn to manage this new life.

At least she would have Elise with her. At the final moment, her mama had relented when Nathaniel had lent his support to her pleas and said, "It's a big step your daughter is taking, Mrs Redfern. It may be of help to have Elise with her while she practises the many skills she has already learned from you."

"Oh, please, Mama," Pretoria had added. "Tamsin will be happy to help you choose a replacement. She would like to have someone nearer her own age, I am sure."

"We both understand it will be a great sacrifice, but we would appreciate it no end," Nathaniel had said.

"Very well. We'll see if Elise is agreeable."

And, of course, she was. "'Tis a lonely step for a girl. She'll settle quicker if I am there," she'd said.

Nathaniel had hired a carriage to transport them to his home, rather than using the chaise. It would be chilly in the open air after dark at this time of year, and he had told his bride she should have everything that was fitting. The first view Pretoria

57

had of her new home was impressive. The tall Elizabethan chimneys were silhouetted against the starry sky, while warm light shone from the windows to greet them. She gasped.

"Is that a pleasurable sound? I do hope so," Nathaniel said.

"It looks warm and friendly," she said, at a loss to add more.

Over the following days there was much that was, indeed, pleasurable, as Pretoria began to experiment with the running of her own house. Elise helped her and the staff were friendly and kind, taking to her leadership with alacrity after having had a master and no mistress for so long.

There were moments she would have preferred her mind to blur as the memory made her feel distressingly ashamed and disloyal. Especially since Nathaniel had made it quite clear he would force her to do nothing with which she was not happy.

That first night, Pretoria lay rigid with embarrassment in her husband's arms, eyes tightly shut. Again, he asked her if he might proceed. He sounded so formal, but she nodded, managing to look at him and smile.

"I don't know what to do," she said in a small voice.

"I will show you. Don't be afraid. It may be uncomfortable the first time, but not thereafter," Nathaniel explained. "Tell me if you want me to stop."

She wasn't frightened at any point, but at first she did pretend that it was Simon's mouth closing upon her own with a velvet touch. It was warm and dry, becoming firm and exploring as her own desires were awoken. They were Simon's hands which caressed her gently, provoking appropriate responses of which she had no previous experience, and which aroused her senses with a highly pleasurable intensity. It was uncomfortable the first time, but the second she enjoyed to the full, and again the next morning. Nathaniel teased her, and she relaxed and giggled; his words lightened the act and made it fun as well as profound.

Pretoria was persuaded to think that the first few days of their time together were more interesting than she had expected, too. Nathaniel escorted her around his estate and introduced her to his tenants. Her natural curiosity was aroused, and she asked questions about crops and husbandry. He answered all of these with seriousness and without signs of amusement at her ignorance of his business.

It was a relief to discover the cook-housekeeper was a motherly soul who happily accepted Elise as the new mistress's maid. The estate manager, Mr Peter Goodwin, lived in a cottage of his own and had served Nathaniel's father. He would retire soon and go to live with his widowed sister, so Nathaniel would need to find another.

Pretoria loved the house. Much of it had been under dust sheets for quite a long time, and Nathaniel was happy for her to open up rooms and order new soft furnishings if she wished. Most of the furniture was carved in dark oak, but it suited the low-ceilinged spaces. The drawing room carpet was a genuine Persian in shades of dark red and gold. Nathaniel had bought it on his travels and had it shipped home. Crimson curtains kept out the chill of the early nights. The morning room was her favourite, for it overlooked the garden and she could step out onto a little terrace by means of French doors. She pictured herself sitting with a hot chocolate or a pot of tea in the early sun in the spring when the flower borders would be more colourful.

Their bedroom was papered in ivory, and she chose primrose muslin for the windows when Nathaniel insisted she update it to suit her taste, rather than retaining the masculine look it had had when she'd arrived. A small dressing room held all her clothes. The heavy double-doored wardrobes continued to house Nathaniel's things, which were not extensive, for he was not a vain man.

Each morning Nathaniel read the newspaper with his meal. Sometimes he would recount the latest to Pretoria, and she listened with concern that equalled his own. She knew the first battle of Ypres just before Christmas had affected him. He'd shared his guilt at sitting at home, when others were engaged in such horrendous acts. "*The defensive firepower of our artillery and machine guns dominate the battlefield*," he read now, "*but the ability of our armies to supply themselves and replace casualties through prolonged battles is becoming more concerning.* I'm increasingly of the mind I should go, my dear. As I've been a member of the Territorial Force since its inception in '08, I think the time is coming for me to sign the Imperial Service Obligation."

"That means you agree to serve overseas, doesn't it?" A sliver of unease slipped down Pretoria's back.

"Yes, that's right. You heard what I read about replacing casualties being difficult. It's people like me they need, my love. I think it's my duty."

"But what of the workers here, the crops and the animals? Surely they need you too, and the Territorial Force was formed to protect *this* country. You've been mobilised and ready for that since last August when war was declared."

"Over there, the need is greater," Nathaniel said simply.

And so it was arranged, with a speed that shook Pretoria. His Imperial Service badge arrived as soon as he had signed his certificate. Then he became part of the First Line or Foreign Service Territorial Forces of the 1st East Lancashire Battalion.

"I shall be training for a short while, but because I've been in the TF and I'm in the middle of my second four-year stint of that, I shall be abroad soon. Apparently people like me, with a little more experience, are needed as officers." There was a hint of excitement in Nathaniel's words, despite Pretoria knowing he was not careless of her emotions. "You'll be alright, my dearest. The staff will look after you, Elise will be here and I will be back in no time at all, but with a clear conscience for having done my bit for King and Empire."

The farewell as her husband left for his weeks of training filled Pretoria with mixed emotions. She was partly relieved at no longer having to pretend emotions she had yet to feel, especially in their bedroom, although she enjoyed the physical aspects of their coming together. However, this relief also made her feel guilty.

When he briefly returned before he left for France, she did not know how she would react.

CHAPTER 10

A week after Nathaniel had left for his training in Colchester, Pretoria received her first letter from him.

My dearest wife,

I couldn't resist writing that. I understand how the circumstances of our marriage have been difficult for you, but know that I love you deeply and will never hurt you.

A gift should be arriving any day now. I know how you love to be free, and I hope this will help. I have been fortunate in acquiring it, as so many have been requisitioned for service overseas. Her name is Miss Hibiscus, and she is a three-year old and roan in colour. Hence the name, I imagine. There, I have probably given the game away. I do hope she helps to pass the time for you.

Tell me of your days if you write to me. I miss my lands, the open countryside and I miss you, my love.

Your affectionate husband,
Nathaniel

The weeks passed slowly at first and then, as the weather warmed, and the horse — Miss Hibiscus — and Pretoria got to know each other, she revelled in her rides across the moors and around the farmland. She often passed the tenants; the women beating rugs or minding young children; one or two older men or teenage boys hoeing the rows of potatoes or driving the cattle in for milking. Although a pair of heavy draught horses had been sent to the depot to be taken to France, they still had a pair of Percherons for heavy ploughing, but that was all done now. The wheat was growing well in its serried rows of blue-green fronds, and Pretoria began to distinguish that from the barley, which was slightly taller and greener at this time of year. She described all this to Nathaniel in a letter.

One day she took her basket and walked down the lane to the little shop to buy a newspaper. In the window was a poster from the National Farmers' Union and a heading that said, 'THE FEW THAT FEED THE MANY'. She had heard and read that the government was becoming concerned about the amount of food that was imported, particularly grains of various types. They had promoted importation for the best part of thirty years in the name of free trade and supporting the Empire. British farms had turned to livestock because they couldn't compete with these foreign import prices. The newspaper she had bought was saying just this. Nathaniel and his estate manager had responded to the call for farmers to increase wheat and other cereal production.

Nathaniel had discussed with her Asquith's Liberal party policy of 'business as usual', believing, as did many, that the war would be over by Christmas. Panic-buying last August and the fact the war was still in progress had changed all that, and new committees were formed to find a solution, although it still involved new contracts for meat with Australia and New Zealand and grain from India. Nathaniel had insisted that the fields of cereal crops were laid down at the back end of the year. Pretoria undertook to discuss this with Peter Goodwin, so she might understand better and support what was happening in her husband's absence.

Nathaniel's second letter detailed some of his training, and it all sounded serious and scary. He wrote, *Today, we had anti-gas instruction and musketry training. We do a lot of marching, too. Tomorrow will be bayonet training and lectures about warfare.* He ended with his love for her and told her he missed their conversations about the work of the estate as well as their more intimate moments.

The personal talk embarrassed Pretoria, and she didn't like the sound of anti-gas at all. She told him of the skylarks she had heard rising from the crop fields, which were growing well in the warm weather. She wrote of new calves and how Mr Goodwin was pleased with progress around the farmlands.

She didn't tell him she loved him for, although she liked him a lot, that stronger emotion eluded her.

Finally, the day came for Nathaniel's return, when he would have forty-eight hours at home before embarkation for France. Pretoria chose her clothing with care, and Elise dressed her hair with woven ribbons the exact same shade of blue as her dress. She sprayed a light perfume, and when she was ready she stood at the window watching for him. She surprised herself by being anxious for his return.

It was late when he finally rode to the front door, swung his leg over and jumped down off his horse, letting the stable lad lead him away before leaping up the front steps, two at a time.

"My love," he said, enfolding her in his arms. "I have longed for this moment."

He smelled of leather and horse, but she discovered she didn't mind. She placed her arms around him in return, thinking she owed him that much, but in fact enjoying the pleasure of giving as well as receiving the warmth and comfort of a hug.

That night he was restrained, the first time. She presumed in deference to her. The second, less so, but Pretoria's body responded in a way that surprised her. The tingling sensations and inner desire were powerful. She had missed him. His caressing fingers made her shiver, raising the hairs on the nape of her neck, and she lifted her chin, luxuriating in the warmth of him. Her breath quickened, and her fingers stroked his hair, his face, his shoulders and back. Her inhibitions dissolved and she became spontaneous to his movements, finally arching her back as they came together with unexpected ecstasy.

Afterwards they lay in each other's arms and Pretoria gave a little laugh at her reckless abandon. Nathaniel kissed her hair. "My darling, it's good, is it not?" He understood.

The next morning, he said, "I have to meet with Peter Goodwin. I should like you to accompany me, if you will. You have shown interest in the estate, and you would be a great help to me while I'm away, I feel sure. Would you do that for me?"

"Really?"

"Yes. You have an enquiring mind, and I do believe Peter would welcome your opinion from time to time."

"It would give me more to do while you are gone," Pretoria said. "Elise and the housekeeper have everything else buttoned up. I should like it very much."

It was settled. Mr Goodwin was a whiskered fellow who reminded Pretoria of her father. His waistcoat stretched over his girth and a thick watchchain hung across the front. Only the top button of his tweed jacket was fastened, as was correct, and it allowed room for his stomach to protrude. He wore a hat that was a cross between a trilby and a fedora, but it was so battered it was hard to tell.

He wasn't tall, and his face had a ruddy glow from the fresh air in which he spent much of his time. A pipe hung from the corner of his mouth, but Pretoria decided it must have gone out. This proved to be the case as he took out some matches and a small tamper and tried, unsuccessfully, to get it to draw. Nevertheless, he replaced it in his mouth.

"Morning, miss. Pleased to have you here." He nodded at her and touched his hat.

Pretoria immediately liked him. She listened while they spoke of acreage, expectations of tonnage, milk yield and how many calves to sell and which to keep. She took it all in and remembered, although when she returned to the house she made notes in a book and popped it in her dressing table drawer for future reference.

When the time came for Nathaniel to leave, Pretoria was genuinely sorry to wave goodbye and wish him God's speed, before he travelled to Southampton and then to Le Havre in France. She wandered around the house after he had gone, picking up and replacing something of his that had fallen to the floor. She folded a woollen jumper and put it to her face, inhaling his scent before she put it away in a drawer. She rearranged his remaining brushes on the chest of drawers, wondering when he would return to use them again.

His first letter arrived a week or so later.

April 5th, 1915
My darling wife,

This is a most strange existence. We are doing a lot of fatigues since I arrived. This means cleaning things that are not yet dirty and marching or playing at killing Germans. Tomorrow we will move to the front line to relieve X. You know I cannot say which battalion we relieve or where we are, precisely. All has been quiet so far.

April 6th

All is quiet again. Rations are different here in the front line, but I am fine. It's variable. Sometimes we have a 'duck's breakfast'. This is a face wash and a drink of water. There seems to be a lot of corned or 'bully' beef from tins, but many of the lads have seen more than enough and, often as not, use it to repair the walls of the trenches. Sometimes there is pork and beans, which is tinned beans with a small cube of pork fat at the bottom. There is also Maconochie, which is a tinned vegetables and meat concoction. It makes a change from the bully. I shall not grow fat. I look forward to a food parcel and cake, or other comforts are welcome, and would not go amiss. One of the lads had Rowntree's clear wine gums, which he shared around. There is a great camaraderie here.

The enemy cannot be far away as snipers are at work, but we keep our heads down. Most of us, anyway. There was a really tall lad, taller even than me. He is no longer with us. I keep reminding the newer lads not to be curious and take a peep over the top of the trench. Curiosity killed the cat, they say.

April 11th

Earlier today the enemy shelled a house. It was only one hundred yards from here, in a coppice, but it was empty, and no one was hurt. They reckon they used shells called whizz bangs. The Boche had a fine time crumping for hours. It gave us a fright because the noise was tremendous, but no harm done. What we really don't like are the minenwerfer. It's a trench mortar and tends to be more accurate. The men call them 'minnies'. Quite a few are duds, though, so there is plenty of souvenir hunting.

Tomorrow we are moving. Perhaps things will get going then, because up until now it has all been routine, more or less, and quiet. Just a good wheeze, really, and I need to be more useful if I am here.

Keep safe, my love. I think of you often.

Your devoted husband,

Nathaniel

It was shortly after this that Pretoria realised she had missed her monthly.

CHAPTER 11

By the end of April, Pretoria was feeling sick each morning. Had it been that last time she had lain with her husband? It must have been. In which case the child would arrive at the end of December. She would wait another month to be certain before letting him know. Not that he could do anything. The news might cheer him, though. She was pleased it was following a time of their coupling that had seemed to mean a little more than previously.

Before he had left they had decided upon a code between them, so she might have some idea of where he was without him writing it, which wasn't allowed. Wheat was France, barley was Belgium and so on.

His next letter gave her a clue.

My dearest darling,

The wheat was not high, but the barley is longer.

We have done a great deal of marching, finally arriving at 3am and digging in fast, which was just as well because the skylarks were flying at dawn.

Clearly it had got past the censors. So, he was in Belgium and German aeroplanes spotters had been about. After reading the newspaper, she guessed he might be somewhere near the town of Ypres. It was a battle there before Christmas that had spurred Nathaniel to sign up for overseas service.

In all the northeast of France and into Belgium, the coal-rich land was of intense interest to both the Germans and the Allies. Ypres also controlled the corridor to the coast of northern France and would set the United Kingdom in the sights of the enemy forces should the town fall into German hands.

It was on here, on 22nd April 1915, that the German forces released one hundred and seventy-one tonnes of chlorine gas along a four-mile stretch of the allied lines.

Pretoria was beside herself with horror and anxiety. She read the newspaper account two days later.

Troops fled in all directions. They were haggard, their overcoats thrown off or wide open, their scarves pulled off and they were running like madmen. They were directionless and calling for water, some rolling on the ground in their efforts to breathe.

The Germans set fire to a chemical product of sulphur chloride which they had placed in front of their own trenches, causing a thick yellow cloud to be blown towards the trenches of the French and Belgians. The cloud of smoke advanced like a yellow low wall, overcoming all those who breathed in the poisonous fumes. The French were unable to see what they were doing or what was happening. The Germans then charged, driving the bewildered French back past their own trenches. Those who were enveloped by the fumes were not able to see each other half a yard apart. I have seen some of the wounded who were overcome by the sulphur fumes, and they were progressing favourably. The effect of the sulphur appears to be only temporary. The after-effects seem to be a bad swelling of the eyes, but the sight is not damaged.

Pretoria was both pleased and excessively guilty when she realised it was French forces who had received the brunt of this attack. In the next moment she thought of all the young men who had wives, mothers and fathers who would be as desperate as she for positive news of a loved one. It was a huge relief to receive Nathaniel's next letter.

Dearest darling,

By now, I'm sure you will have heard of the awful attack on the wheat fields near us. We knew something was up when we couldn't get past on the road for the number of refugees. We went along the railway line and saw several soldiers lying there in a terrible state and one said it was gas. I had heard of this on my training, but I'd never imagined what it meant. Back then, it was all quite a laugh when we had to wear cloth head coverings and they talked of soaking them in urine, which we thought was them having a joke with us. I do believe our laughter was a release of tension and perhaps even a touch hysterical.

I will not recount the effect of the gas in reality, but it was vastly different to training. It is too horrible for you to even contemplate, my dearest. Suffice to say it did not reach our section. If this gets past the censor, it will be because they want those at home to know for what we are fighting. The barbarity of that attack was unbelievable.

Know that I love you and wish I could hold you close and smell your perfume to erase that odour which is permanently with me here. Please write soon and give me some good news of our estates, but more of you, my love.

Your loving husband,
Nathaniel xx

Pretoria sat at the writing desk in the morning room where the sun streamed in. She looked out at the flower borders where spring plants bobbed their yellow and blue heads in the breeze and where the primroses formed little pale cushions of colour. She could not compare her view with the horror she had read about, the details of which she could only imagine.

Dear Nathaniel,

It is hard to comprehend what you have told me and the things I have read in the newspapers here.

I do have some news for you, and I hope it will help you to see that we wait to welcome you home with immense anticipation. I am with child. Yes, it's true and it should be born in December. I have been a little under the weather in the mornings, but I am assured by Elise and Mama that it will soon pass.

Surely all this horror must be over by then. We thought it would have been done by last Christmas, so I have every confidence it will be over by the next one, when there will be three of us to celebrate.

In other news, the crops are growing well. Peter and I walked the fields last week and I have visited the tenants' cottages with him. Mrs Beale is with child, too. How she manages with three children under the age of five and another coming, I do not know. I will ensure they all have enough to eat, but the eggs and milk help, of course.

Please do take care and come home safely.

Your wife,

Pretoria

CHAPTER 12

At the end of the following month Tamsin came to stay for two weeks by herself, Mama not being able to get away from the department store. She brought messages and gifts from their parents, and it was lovely to see her after their months apart. While she was still uninterested in her clothing and general appearance, she had grown taller and had a good figure.

"You'll never guess who Mama has employed to help me with my daily tasks," she said. "I made the suggestion, but after Mama spoke with Mrs Strong all was settled."

"Now you have me guessing. You must tell all."

"It's Gisela."

"The daughter of Izzy's German teacher, Frau Schröder? Well, I am surprised. Didn't Mama mind that she's, well … German?"

"I did have to plead with her, but really there was no one else. It's such a good solution."

"I thought the neighbours gave the mother some odd glances when I last visited and went to church with all of you. I did think local people were none too friendly about her, so frankly, I'm amazed."

"Initially Mama said it would be for a trial period and we would find someone else as soon as possible, but in reality she has moved on and is immersed in her work at the store." Tamsin giggled.

"I hope you will not be bored here alone with us," Pretoria said.

"No, not at all."

Later, Pretoria confided to Elise, "She is so clever, she may find us dull when I am sitting sewing baby clothes."

"She will enjoy the freedom," Elise said, "and you could take her shopping. Buy her a new dress in a more becoming colour. Tell your mama that Mr Nathaniel said you should, and she will be more than happy."

After discussing the idea with Tamsin, they decided they would take the trap to the station and catch the train into Manchester. Elise would accompany them, and they would make a whole day of it, taking coffee at the Kardomah Café in Market Street. It was a rare outing, and they were both excited.

It was here they were sitting, soaking up the delicious aroma and watching all the people around them as they waited to be served, when Mrs Margaret Parks spotted them. She weaved her way between the tables. Pretoria groaned at the sight of her and then managed to paste on a smile. The woman came towards them with a smirk on her painted face, before delighting in giving Pretoria two major shocks.

"My dears, how lovely to see you both. You look positively blooming, Pretoria, and Tamsin is growing up now. Such a pretty hat," she added, looking at Tamsin's straw monstrosity which they were about to replace. She turned to Elise. "And you are…? Oh, the maid. Good-day."

Pretoria stirred herself to be polite without encouraging the woman. "I hope you're keeping well."

"Yes, indeed, although the social scene is not what it was, is it? So many men away and things as they are. I did go to the Harrisons' the other night. Everyone who is anyone was there, of course, although I didn't see you, my dear Pretoria."

"No, I chose not to accept the invitation under the circumstances of the war, and Nathaniel being away fighting. It didn't seem quite the thing." She couldn't resist the final barb but was then sorry for lowering herself to this woman's level.

"Mm, well, I did see Julia Worthington, so it's probably just as well you and Mr Moore were not there. She is separated from the man she left him for, Lord Doddington. Told me confidentially, of course, that she regretted her error. It would be quite a *faux pas* to invite them both to the same party, I believe." She gave a titter. "But then, I'm sure your Nathaniel is happy to have married you. He certainly did so quickly after that other business."

Pretoria had a premonition and she sat very still. All she could see was this woman's bright red lips as they moved. She had lipstick on her large front teeth. Then her words penetrated as she prattled on, knocking Pretoria sideways.

"Simon Rashbrooke was there. You could have pushed me down when he walked in, as bold as you like. He was in uniform. Home on leave or for further training, I suppose, and he didn't stay long. He even had the effrontery to speak to me."

Pretoria glanced at her companions and saw compassion in Elise's eyes.

"Have you seen him, my dear? He had the impertinence to enquire after you."

"No, I have no wish to hear of him, Mrs Parks." Pretoria's heart was thumping hard, and she feared this horrid woman would see her distress.

Mrs Parks carried on regardless. "No, I suppose not. Still, with Mr Moore away … you never know. He asked me to convey his good wishes, should I see you. He is as handsome as ever, of course. Those eyes, so blue, but I'm sure you are able to picture them. After all, you were so close, weren't you?"

Pretoria grew dizzy and her fingers tingled.

"Well, I better be going. Have a lovely day, ladies. Give my good wishes to your husband when you eventually see him. I hope he doesn't bump into Julia. That could be awkward, I think." She tittered again, waved her fingers in an artificial manner, straightened her Victorian fur wrap with its head and legs dangling, which Pretoria thought was vulgarly ostentatious, and left.

Elise breathed out and reached for the coffee pot to pour for all three of them. "Right, my loves," she said with briskness, "forget all that. She's a foolish empty-headed person who has no sense and no feelings. Let's plan the next part of our day. Where shall we shop for a hat for Miss Tamsin?"

The excitement for the day had left Pretoria, and she was in turmoil with much to think about, but she made a gigantic effort to pull her mind away from all she had learned and smiled, just a little too broadly, at her sister. "Ooh, Tammy. This will be such an adventure. What colour shall we look for?"

By the time they got home it was late, and Pretoria was exhausted both mentally and physically. She bade them goodnight and retreated to her bedroom at the first opportunity, but although tired she could not relax. Her mind was buzzing.

What if she bumped into Simon? Did she want to? And what of Julia Worthington? Would she begin to pursue Nathaniel when he returned, or would he chase her? Probably not. She had hurt him immeasurably. In his letters, he told her he loved only her and would never hurt her. Was that the truth? Would he still say that when he knew the truth of current matters with his previous love?

She placed her hand over her stomach. This little one would change things, too. She must write to Nathaniel and discuss names with him. She would do that in the morning, she decided, and put other thoughts from her.

A small tap at her door made her sit up. It cracked open and Elise's round face peered in. She entered holding a cup. "Hot milk with a spoon of honey. Remember how that used to soothe when you were little? I thought it might be welcome now."

"Dear Elise," Pretoria said. "You are always so wise and know exactly what I need."

Elise placed the cup on the little table at the side of the bed, and as she sat down near the end there was a gentle bounce. "I bet you have thoughts whirling around inside that pretty head of yours."

Pretoria breathed out in a gust. "Yes. A little."

"I knew it. You can hide nothing from old Elise. I would say this, though. Pay no heed at all to that excuse for a female. She has no empathy at all. She prefers to get a reaction from any old gossip, whether it's based in truth or not. You are in a good situation here, and Mr Moore thinks the world of you. Everyone can see that." She stood, picked up the cup and placed it in Pretoria's hands. "Now drink that, and then snuggle down for a good night's rest."

"You sound as you did when I woke with nightmares as a child. Thank you, dear Elise."

Pretoria did as she was told, then, turning out the light, she lay for a while, remembering Nathaniel and the things they had done together that last night, probably when their baby had been conceived. She cupped her stomach and smiled into the dark.

At last, her eyelids drooped.

Pretoria and Elise returned with Tamsin to her family home, intending to stay for only a week or so. It was strange for Pretoria to be back, after running her own home with reasonable success. Mama expected she would slot back in to all the routines, but it was hard. She missed her daily rides on Miss Hibiscus, and she was bored, so she decided to take the omnibus into town and have a look around the family's department store as a diversion.

While there, she bumped into Rose Strong. Pretoria had always appreciated her calm friendship.

"Have you time to take a cup of coffee with me? To be honest, I'm not ready to go back to Mama and Papa's house yet," she told Rose.

"That would be lovely, and you must tell me all about your new life, although it must be hard without your husband by your side," Rose said.

As they sat in the Summer Court tearoom in the store, Pretoria had a desire to share her troubles with someone who, she knew instinctively, would understand.

"Is something troubling you, my dear?" Rose asked.

"You always were the intuitive one when we were children," Pretoria answered. She hesitated and then shared what Margaret Parks had told her.

"I did see Simon here, as it happens. We nodded at each other but didn't speak. I understand he has returned to the front line now. Would you have seen him if the opportunity arose?"

Again, Pretoria hesitated.

"Maybe he would have altered his outlook and left behind his gambling ways, but who knows? There is still the other matter of his wife."

Rose looked at her and pushed her glasses further up her nose before saying, "I understand there was a child, too."

"So I gather."

"Too many complications would not have been easy to cope with, dear Pretoria. Some ways cannot be changed and even if they could, other things make too many issues and must be managed by the architect. That was Simon Rashbrooke. There are responsibilities that cannot be evaded. Sometimes we see things as we would like them to be rather than how they actually are." Rose reached out and touched Pretoria's hand. "Be contented, Preti," she said, using the childhood nickname. "You have a good man in Nathaniel, who adores you from what I have seen. We must all be thankful for what we have, especially at the moment. "

"You're right, of course."

"Have you heard from Michael?" Rose asked. "Your mama must be worried for your brother over in France."

"She is, but I think she works on the principle that no news is a good thing." Pretoria looked closely at Rose. Was she asking for a more personal reason?

They finished their refreshments and Pretoria thanked Rose for her advice. "Somehow it helps to talk things over," she said. "Tamsin is too young and Mama, well, I can't share it with her."

"And how is Tamsin? She and Izzy seem to get on so well, but I haven't seen her in ages."

"She seems in good health, but very restless, Mama says. She does keep talking of war work, but she seems so young, and I don't know what she would do. She wouldn't survive in a munitions factory." Pretoria frowned.

"That's awful work indeed, and the girls who do that are to be admired. I thought at one time it was all that would be left for me to do, when Delphi joined the Women's Legion. My eyesight would not pass muster. Fortunately, I found the office work I do for the Ministry in Manchester. It's difficult sometimes, arranging things for the relatives of those missing or who have lost their lives at the front, but I think I'm of use."

Pretoria thought of all the different worries and problems this war had created. She sighed.

"Perhaps Tamsin could come and stay with you for a while," Rose suggested. "I'm sure your mama wouldn't mind her being away from the store."

"She just came for a few days, but maybe she could come for longer. I think that's a good idea. Thank you, Rose. You have put my mind at ease in several ways."

CHAPTER 13

July 1915
The wheatfields are growing and we must move with the times, Nathaniel
wrote.

So, he had moved to somewhere in France.

*Several of our Company had to go to hospital with a sickness, but I'm
as strong as ever and soldiering on, as the saying goes. A captain named
Phillips blew off his thumb and two fingers of his right hand, attempting to
un-charge the detonator of a hand grenade. His misfortune is my good
luck, but that's how it goes out here. I heard the fellow will recover and
return soon. I hope so. I liked him a lot. I've received a promotion so must
struggle to sew on the insignia when we return to rest.*

*I miss you, my darling. Something happened here, which I was not going
to mention, but think I owe it to you to tell. It brought out the worst, and
then maybe the best of me, so here it goes.*

*We took a heavy bombardment and one of our companies suffered
badly. Not mine. Then the enemy's infantry attacked but were driven off
by a Company to our right. The breastworks of the trenches were severely
damaged by the shelling, so when all was quiet again we set to mend them.
I had to detail some men to go over the top into no man's land for this
task. This meant crawling across the mud, and there I came across
someone you know. Simon Rashbrooke. He was injured in the shoulder,
had a bad leg wound and had lost a lot of blood.*

*This is where the worst of me came in. I hesitated and watched him for
five minutes while he lay there in a sort of coma, I imagine. He was
covered in mud, of course. I'm sorry if this distresses you. I know how you
feel for him, still, I think. I was sorely tempted to leave him there, the*

worthless wretch. I could tell you he died in my arms and that there was nothing I could do. I could lead you to think I was covered in humanity in my care for him, when all I wanted was for him to be gone. Or I could deny all knowledge, and if he died there, he would be covered with mud and decay into this hellish nightmare during the next shelling, and none would be the wiser. In the end, he opened his eyes. I gave him the last of my water. I had my own First Field Dressing pack. It's not much; two rolled bandages with gauze wadding and an iodine capsule and safety pins. I was able to patch him with those, and then managed to haul him back into the trench, where I called the stretcher bearers. Be consoled, my dear. They would have taken him to a field dressing station and on to hospital. I'm sure he will live, if only to fight again. That is the way here for those who are wounded. They are patched up in order to return to the fighting, but at least he lives, for the moment.

Even now, I despair that if he had not opened his eyes at that moment and looked at me, would I have acted as I finally did? I hope I did this for you, my dearest. How could I look into your eyes again if I had acted basely and left him there to die in agony? How could I face you with my honest love if I didn't have a clear conscience?

Despite all these conflicts of emotion that I have had, I trust you will not think too badly of me, because my love for you will never diminish.

I remain your loving husband,
Nathaniel xx

As Pretoria read this account, and then read it again, she had mixed emotions herself. Her first thoughts were for the wounded Simon. She had difficulty picturing his face at all, and certainly could not hear his voice.

Then she thought about Nathaniel confessing his basest thoughts to her on first finding his nemesis. Did she think badly of her husband for his temptation to leave his rival to rot in a foreign place? She plonked down onto the bed to think it through. It was hard to imagine the circumstances, although she knew there was mud and shell holes and no greenery for miles. He had told her that much before, in his letters, and asked her to share the sights, sounds and scents of her surroundings, so he might imagine himself back at home in the sweet-scented greenery.

When all was considered, she didn't think badly of Nathaniel. In fact, a small ray of pride threaded its way through her veins. That he would be so honest with her was something at which to marvel. He had morality and integrity. He had overcome his initial desires and saved a wretch. She was proud of him and pleased to call herself his wife.

Pretoria's stomach was swelling now, and she had experienced the first flutter of movement. To begin with, she was unsure. It was like a tiny flick of a finger inside her. Then another similar sensation made her marvel at it. This child was real.

As she grew larger, Tamsin came to stay, and brought her companion Gisela with her. Pretoria still met with Peter Goodwin and often Tamsin came too, and they both tried to improve their understanding of the estate and its workings. This was something small Pretoria could do for Nathaniel so that when he finally returned, his business would be in good shape. The new President of the Board of Agriculture was a more progressive thinker, apparently, and when she discussed it with Peter, he confirmed her view.

"I read he is taking steps to assess how the country could increase food production, assuming that the war continues past the 1916 harvest," Pretoria said.

"Quite right, my dear. You understand this situation well, I see."

She was gratified, and when she glanced at Tamsin, her sister grinned and nodded her approval.

"We must restore things to arable cultivation and return the poorer grassland to cereal production. There's talk of guaranteeing a price, which will make all the difference."

"We have that land in the top fields over there. Can't we do something with that? Maybe plant winter wheat or oats, even, in the late autumn?"

"Clever lass. Yes. Oats would be perfect up there. May I have a quiet word, miss?" Peter glanced at Tamsin.

The younger girl took the hint and said, "I'll say good day to you, Mr Goodwin, and thank you for a most interesting morning."

Peter looked awkward.

"You may say whatever is on your mind, Peter. I shall not take offence." Pretoria sought to put him at his ease.

He paused and then took a deep breath. "It's just that there's talk among the farm workers, miss."

"Talk?"

He pulled a face as if in pain. "It grieves me to say this, for she is but a young lass."

"Who, Tamsin?"

"No, miss, the other one. The one who is her companion or whatever."

"Oh, Gisela."

"Yes, miss. She's a German, you see."

"Ah!" Pretoria understood.

"I'm alright with it, of course. She just a girl, but there are some who are whispering among themselves, and I fear for her, you see."

"Thank you, Peter. I'm grateful to you for putting me in the picture."

"I'm right sorry, miss. I'm sure she's not a spy or anything, but…"

"Please, it's fine. I'm glad you've said it."

That afternoon, Pretoria rode out on Miss Hibiscus and Tamsin borrowed an ancient pony from the stable. It was good for her mind, to be out on the hills and away from everything. It gave her a chance to think. Elise was decidedly unhappy about her riding out, but before she left Pretoria said, "I shall only walk her. She needs the exercise, as do I. We shall come to no grief. Tamsin will come, too."

While she was out, she relished the breeze in her hair as she pushed her hat to the back of her head, and it hung by its strap around her neck. As she tilted her head, the sun was warm on her face, and she was refreshed. There was nothing quite so beautiful as these hills on a late summer's day.

While the horse walked, Pretoria had the rhythm of it running through her, and she thought of the advice that Rose Strong had given her, and the things Nathaniel had said in his last letter. He was a good man and she hoped he was safe.

Finding a suitable rock to help her, she dismounted. Miss Hibiscus nuzzled her rounded stomach, and Pretoria and her sister let the animals crop as best they might. Together, the girls lay on short, spiky grass and gazed into the blue.

"Look at that," Tamsin said, pointing above her.

A buzzard hung above them, circling on a thermal which gathered and rose over the hill. Then it was joined by a second one. A mate? She heard their shrill, plaintive call to each other. All of a sudden, tears coursed down her cheeks. She dashed them away before Tamsin could ask questions. She was lonely. She missed Nathaniel. She missed their shared jokes and laughter, she missed his arms around her. She missed his lips on hers and their lovemaking, which was empathy and celebration as well as passion.

Pretoria turned her attention to her sister and was about to bring up the subject of which Peter had spoken earlier, when Tamsin said, "I think both Gisela and I should like to join the Women's Land Army."

CHAPTER 14

Life progressed. Letters were exchanged, meetings with Peter Goodwin about estate matters continued, tenants were visited, and running the household, depleted as it was, carried on. Tamsin had been persuaded to think more about her latest desire. Pretoria was convinced it was a romantic fad.

In the middle of December, Tamsin had returned to her own home and Pretoria was bored with enforced inactivity. She spent a happy morning re-hanging her dresses in colour order, emptying her underwear drawer, and re-folding all her garments and putting them back. She didn't feel like eating any lunch, but Elise said she must have something. Cook tempted her with a portion of chicken and potato she had mashed with butter and a little spoonful of rich cream. After Pretoria had managed a small bowl of flummery flavoured with a light elderflower pressé, she went to her room to lie down. She had an achy feeling in her back, so she turned on her side and placed a pillow beneath her bulging stomach for support. Sometime later, the pain came again, and then again, but this time spreading below her bump. It suddenly dawned on her she might have started her labour, although it was a little earlier than she had thought. She waited. There it was again.

The confinement was longer than expected, and hard. All through that afternoon and evening, Pretoria struggled with the pain. Dr Madison arrived and declared nothing was ready to happen yet, and still Pretoria rolled her head, trying to control a moan as the wave overtook her again. Elise's presence at her bedside did more to comfort her and give her courage than anything the doctor or midwife said or did. She vaguely heard the doctor say to the midwife, "I think it's time for the hyoscine and morphine now." He turned to Pretoria. "A little twilight sleep will help you now, mother."

The child was born at three o'clock the following morning, and Pretoria fell into a deep slumber and was not aware of what followed.

Later she awoke once, in an extremely confused state, and thought Nathaniel was kneeling beside her, his face hidden in the covers. His shoulders appeared to heave, and she thought he was weeping, but then she drifted off again. The next time she came to, she thought it was silly that she was so limp and weak, but she managed to put out her hand and feel his hair. It was real. Was he really there? She was confused, but at her touch he raised his head to look at her. Never had she seen him so haggard and drawn. He took her hand and pressed her palm to his lips, before whispering in an unfamiliar hoarse tone, "You are back with me? My darling, how are you?"

"I'm so tired, so weak and feeble. Nathaniel, dear, we have a son, I believe."

"We have. I've seen him and he's beautiful. He's a perfect little human being." He kissed her palm again and laid his cool hand on her forehead.

With sleep clouding her mind again, Pretoria managed to say, half teasingly, "I have done my duty, husband. You have an heir for your estate." She sank into warm, smothering darkness again.

Pretoria's recovery from her confinement was delayed. She was amazed to learn she had almost lost her life from a rare haemorrhage, and the doctor said she must take things very slowly. She understood now that it was coincidence that Nathaniel had come home on leave on that very night. He had been sent for three weeks to attend a further training course in

Manchester, but he could live at home and travel daily. He wouldn't say exactly what it was for, but hinted it was to do with a new type of explosive. Upon his return, he would not be going back to France but to a different front line. He vaguely mentioned Ypres in Belgium but would not speak definitively. She knew he had a dread of that place, but he would not be questioned on it and certainly did not want to share anything about what it might involve.

Pretoria had to remain in bed, which was frustrating. As she lay sleepily, two mornings later, she remembered that just along the hallway Master Arthur Moore would probably be bawling for some food. At that moment, the door opened and Nathaniel came into the room, looking only slightly less haggard than when she'd last seen him. He swore the baby had had enough milk from her while she slept and that he would thrive. Of this she had no recollection.

"Where did you sleep?" she asked him. "You look so tired." She was slightly disconsolate that he'd stayed somewhere else that night and worried where that might have been, until he told her he had slept on a truckle bed downstairs.

"I'm used to it." He laughed mirthlessly and Pretoria was ill at ease. He seemed distant from her.

Over the next two days, Nathaniel's demeanour continued to concern her. She could not quite see what it was, but since the night of the baby's birth she'd sensed a difference in him; a kind of restraint that hadn't been there before he'd gone away. Then, they had been developing a comfortable intimacy and his letters had been loving. He was gently solicitous, still kind, but something had indefinably changed.

Of course, they were rarely alone. Elise was there, her mother visited for two days, friends called in to meet the new member of the family and bring gifts. At night Nathaniel came to the bedroom, sat for a while, and talked about the estate or his activities during the day, but there was a reserve that puzzled her.

If they had been much in love, as a normal couple, she would have questioned him, but shyness and pride restrained her. Theirs had been a marriage of expediency. In the first weeks of their time together, he had not said he loved her, but in many of his letters he had. She was not surprised by his lack of ardent vocalisation. Theirs was a coupling of friendly understanding rather than loving passion, apart from their moments of lovemaking, but since that first night back at home he hadn't even taken her hand or kissed her goodnight.

She tried to ask him about his experiences, wondering if that was the reason for his reticence, but while he didn't tell her all the gruesome details, he told her enough for her to know he was coping with the dirt and noise and smells of trench life as well as seeing some of his companions lose their lives.

Christmas came and went and two of Nathaniel's three weeks at home passed. Pretoria was out of bed, but still not working to her full capacity. Nathaniel came into the morning room as she sat. "It's good to see you downstairs and dressed. How are you feeling? I looked in to see our baby. I couldn't resist. He seems to have grown already."

"Yes, he is flourishing, and I am stronger by the day."

"I cannot stay. Duty calls." And he was gone for the day's training.

Baby Arthur was feeding well, and although he seemed to cry a lot, Elise was on hand to help while Nathaniel took up some of the estate work with Peter when he wasn't in Manchester. All too soon his time was up, and he had to return to the Continent.

On the morning of his departure, he held the child and Pretoria thought she saw his eyes fill as he kissed him. She would miss him, despite his reticence of late. He kissed her cheek like a brother, which distressed her, and told her not to overdo things, and then he was away down the drive. He turned and waved before he disappeared around the bend and into the lane.

A few days later, Pretoria was sitting in the morning room. She had her legs up on the settee and was taking advantage of Arthur having a sleep at last.

She heard voices and recognised Elise's distinct tones. "I'm not sure if she is at home, ma'am."

"Ah. The estate manager I passed on my way up the drive assured me she was. I would love to see the child, as I've come all this way."

"Yes. I'll go and see. We weren't expecting visitors."

Elise appeared in the doorway, looking grim. "It's that awful Mrs Parks. I tried to put her off," she whispered.

Pretoria swung her legs down and sat up straighter. Elise showed the visitor in, then left to fetch baby Arthur.

"Mrs Parks. Forgive my state. I wasn't expecting anyone and I'm still a little weak." She wasn't, but she didn't need this person to stay for long.

"I simply had to come after talking with your mama and hearing how poorly you have been. Ah, here is the little fellow."

"Thank you, Elise." Pretoria took her son.

After tea was brought and poured, and all the appropriate noises had been made over the child, Margaret Parks turned to what Pretoria guessed was the real reason for her visit. She started with a preamble of empty chatter about shared acquaintance. "I hear that homely cousin of Mr Parkington is to be married. Such a surprise. I imagine you have not heard all the latest, shut away as you are. Do you remember Maud Hatch? Maud Lawson, as was. Went to live in India?"

"Yes, we were friends for a while." Pretoria wondered what cheering thing was coming next out of this dreadful woman's mouth.

"Well, she and her husband had a terrible carriage accident. So sad, both of them killed."

"Oh dear. That *is* awful news. In India?"

"Yes. Their child is left all alone. No relatives, I understand." Mrs Parks rattled on. Pretoria switched off as she remembered Maud, a kind and gentle lass. "It must have been a comfort to have your dear husband at home. He looked so healthy, too. Lucky man. I saw him at the little soirée Mrs Pollard held a couple of weeks ago. So good to see him laughing with Julia Worthington. He seems to have forgiven her for her harsh treatment of him, but you must know that. We were sorry you were unable to come with your husband."

So that's why she came, Pretoria thought, as the heat of anger and anxiety raked through her. "I haven't been going out yet," she said.

"No, quite. Still, as I say, it was good to see Nathaniel enjoying himself when he was expecting to return to the Continent. I'm sure he needed the light relief that Julia was able to give him."

It seemed good fortune when Arthur stirred and began to cry. Pretoria was able to shield her gaze by looking down at him, and without further comment she said, "I think he is hungry. You must forgive me." She stood.

Her visitor had to leave her cup of tea half drunk. Elise, bless her, arrived to escort Mrs Parks out.

CHAPTER 15

Pretoria missed Nathaniel. Before he'd gone abroad the first time, she'd started to become accustomed to his gentle teasing; his good common sense when coping with her mother; his explanations concerning things about the estate; and, yes, his lovemaking, which was full of care for her. He managed to arouse her senses and even indulged his own zeal.

The more she thought about his restraint since the birth of their son, the more she worried. Perhaps it was because she had been so ill, and he didn't want to risk her health again. But if he had re-encountered Julia Worthington, perhaps he was pining for her, although his diffidence had started before the date of that soirée, surely.

She vacillated between one theory and another, until one afternoon Elise questioned her. "You seem out of sorts these days. Are you fretting for Mr Moore? He has been safe so far, you know, and I'm sure he will not be careless of himself or his Company. Especially not now he has you and the child, an heir."

Pretoria sighed and paused while she wondered whether to confide in Elise. "I do worry about his safety, of course, but ... Mrs Parks told me something."

"Ah, Mrs Parks. Why she had to come here spreading her horrid gossip, I don't know. Tell me, then. You know a problem shared is a problem halved."

Pretoria told her all that had passed.

"That wretched woman. Pardon me," Elise said. "She spreads nothing but idle rubbish, and you should have more sense than to listen to it, child. He loves you. I'm sure of it."

"Perhaps he has found peace and comfort with someone else while he has been here. Julia, maybe, whom he wanted so much at one time. It wouldn't be the first time such a thing has happened to a man and his wife, who must bear it, somehow."

"Stuff and nonsense," Elise said.

"I heard she is free again and, according to Mrs Parks, more careless of conventions than ever. She was called cold and ruthless, before. And while it has not been mentioned since we married, Nathaniel knows how I had hopes of being with Simon Rashbrooke. Julia was always beautiful and elegant. Perhaps he thinks he might as well follow his heart again."

"Surely you have a greater opinion of him than you are suggesting. Think of what you are accusing him of, and then decide if he would fall for such a thing."

When Nathaniel's next letter arrived, it was with shock that she read his news, especially since Simon had been on her mind so much.

Dearest Pretoria,

You will know from conversations we had before I left that I have been in the wheat fields all this time. Things have not been good, but I am well, and so far we are managing with what we have. I could do with some woollen socks, next time you are knitting, although the weather is getting better. These comforts are so much more than they might seem to those who send them. The mud never goes, but the duckboards are less slippery.

I cannot put the next bit off any longer. I have some news to impart, and this time I had no hand in it. None at all, I assure you.

We have taken some heavy shelling, and although you could say we are winning the battle, it's hard to see how that is so. We have hardly moved in weeks. Anyway, someone you once knew well was hit and, I cannot say this more gently, Simon Rashbrooke has been killed. I was nowhere near, but I heard the news.

Pretoria dropped the letter as her heart pounded. She sat stiffly upright, remembering him. *He was charming, probably ruthless, a gambler, a risk-taker.* It had been likely to happen. Curiously, while she was upset that such life and vitality had been cut short, she was not torn asunder, as once she would have been. The tragedy was his. He had become careless of others, including her in the end. And now he had probably been careless of himself and paid the highest price.

She considered what life with him would have been like, and compared it to her situation now. She had happiness here: her little son and Nathaniel.

Nathaniel was cramped in this front-line trench, sheltering in a dugout. Previously soaking wet and freezing cold, it was now sultrily hot and airless. He was supposed to be writing his report, but he was distracted. He'd already been here for ten days, so they were due to be relieved soon and could move to a rear reserve position. He scratched his chest. He'd managed to avoid the cholera and had had only one bout of dysentery. He hadn't told Pretoria about that. No one could avoid the lice, though, or the rats for that matter. Rat hunting, or rat bashing, was one of the 'sports' in which the men indulged frequently, when things were quiet. It took their minds off the flies. But he wouldn't think further of those, or the reasons why there were so many of the vile rodents.

He'd have to get up in a minute and struggle along the narrow trench to keep his men awake. They'd had all day to sleep in a bolthole, if they could, or hunker down against the trench wall. Now it was late evening, when the action was likely to start.

He'd written to Pretoria three days ago, so she should have received his letter by now. At least the post was good.

Will Simon now be a martyr in her eyes? He wondered. His thoughts continued as he tapped the end of his pencil against his knee. *She's already said she has done her duty by me and produced an heir.* He remembered his words to her in the park the day he had given her his proposition. *'An heir will be part of the arrangement, but once it is accomplished, I will not trouble you further.' And I didn't, although I wanted desperately to lie beside her and enfold her in my arms. I was frightened if I kissed her I would not be able to stop.*

The thought of losing her, as he almost had, made him squeeze his eyes tightly shut and his mouth went dry. His hand holding the pencil trembled and he threw it down. He'd have to finish the report later. He must be careful. Lack of concentration was one of the greatest dangers. That's when foolish mistakes were made. A head held too high, a sound missed that could mean the enemy creeping forwards.

He remembered a couple of weeks ago when he had bumped into Michael Redfern, Pretoria's older brother. He, too, had feigned happiness, speaking of those at home in overly bright tones, but he'd drank too much that night, striving to forget what was missing from his life. They were all the same: aching, struggling, and pining, but desperately suppressing it.

He stood and bent his head. The trench was narrow, and he had to step over the bodies of sleeping men. He'd wake them on his way back. In one place the duckboard was missing — it had probably got wacked by a direct hit at some point. Some lags had filled the space with the tins of bully beef that none of them were keen on. They'd tasted so much of it. Still, sometime soon they should be able to get to the village and maybe even have an omelette in the little café. His mouth watered at the thought. Such small pleasures were what kept them all going in this hell hole.

It was hard to remain sane. One week they were all sitting around or being kept busy artificially, with fatigues, drill and cleaning equipment, and the next week was manic noise, horror, blood and events too nightmarish to share. It all had to be buried and kept from those at home. And there he was again. Those at home …

CHAPTER 16

At home, Pretoria was sitting on the terrace in the shade. It was a hot and humid day. She rocked her child as she wondered what Nathaniel was doing and prayed he was safe. These days she tried hard to quash all her anxieties by throwing herself into the estate business as well as looking after Arthur. He was a fretful baby, and she often wondered if it was because she was ill at ease much of the time. Although letters came regularly, the lapse between Nathaniel writing and her receiving them was always a worry. In those few days, anything might have happened.

Elise appeared through the French doors to tell her a person wished to speak with her, and her alone. Her expression was affronted, to say the least.

Puzzled, Pretoria said, "What kind of person?"

"An elderly woman. She gave her name as Mrs Lucy Harris, if you like, but refused to state her business."

"The name means nothing to me."

"She told me she has travelled all the way from Norfolk. She doesn't look at all well, so what she is after, who knows. She's insisting on seeing you personally, on some urgent matter." Elise shrugged to indicate she believed none of it.

"How very strange."

"She asked me to give you this." Elise held out a sealed paper and huffed as Pretoria stood, handed over Arthur and took it.

Pretoria's heart seemed to fly into her throat. She knew this writing. She wanted to sit again, to collapse into the chair she had just vacated. Elise's expression changed from exasperation to frowning concern.

Pretoria ran through the French doors, clutching the paper. She had only seen the handwriting once or twice previously and here it was, come back from the dead to haunt her.

Mrs Nathaniel Moore,
Private.
c/o Mrs Lucy Harris.
To be delivered by hand in the event of my death.

The handwriting was that of Simon Rashbrooke.

"Mrs Harris?" The woman wore a black coat and a black straw hat with the same colour ribbon around it. Both looked as ancient as she did. Her iron-grey hair was wispy and there were beads of sweat along her top lip as she stood, one hand holding the doorframe to steady herself. "Please, come this way." Pretoria ushered the woman to the drawing room and was careful to close the door. She indicated a seat and sat opposite. Mrs Harris was panting. "May I offer you a cold drink? It's so hot today."

"No, thank you, ma'am." Mrs Harris sank back onto the cushions with evident relief.

"Are you unwell? I can call someone." Pretoria looked at the pale puffy face and noted her lips were a little too blue.

"No, ma'am. I shall do well for sitting. Thank you, ma'am. 'Tis my 'eart 'as bin a bit troublesome of late. I shall do fine in a minute."

Pretoria waited, biting her lip and controlling her impatience, while her companion's breathing slowed. "Take your time," she said. "I understand you wish to speak with me, and you have brought me this." She held up the letter, still sealed. After some minutes, when Mrs Harris seemed more relaxed, Pretoria continued, "Are you able to tell me what you want, now?"

"I do think it best you read the letter, ma'am. I think 'twill explain better than I, what it is 'e wants. I've 'ad it for some months but now it's yours."

"Very well." Pretoria broke the seal. For a moment, the script danced before her eyes. Bittersweet memories flooded her mind until, with an effort, she concentrated on the words before her.

June 30th, 1916

Pretoria, my dearest and beloved,

I know I have no right to use those words but if you are reading this, it is because I have left this world, and so what do the things I have done matter anymore? What is important is that I ensure the future is better than the past.

First, I must ask, no, implore, your forgiveness. I was cruel and cowardly. If you are reading this, I hope I have died with greater courage than I lived with. It is better that I am gone, if that is so, for I was selfish and did some unpardonable things, not least to you. I loved you. I truly did, but should not have done, as you will surely know by now, since I was not free.

Tears surged. Pretoria glanced at Mrs Harris before reading on.

Perhaps you loved me a little, too. I have endured anguish since I left you. The life here in France is unimaginable to those at home, and on top of that I live with many regrets. The whole of the county must know what I have done, but there are other things I wish you alone to know. I am married, it is true; my wife and I are both of the Catholic faith and therefore are unable to divorce. I was only eighteen when we wed, and because she was about to bear my child, I undertook the obligation. She is some years older than I, and for a while I was enslaved. That time in my life was also a chance for me to escape an abusive childhood living with a drunkard father after my mother died.

I soon found my wife to be intensely possessive, although I did not ease the situation with my roaming and philandering. Yes, even then, to my shame. She is passionately jealous, and we had terrible quarrels when she accused me of deceits and cruelties. I am trying to be honest: some of those accusations may be true, though not all. One day during a particularly loud and violent argument, she seized a kitchen knife and sliced my shoulder. I believe she was aiming for my heart, and perhaps she should have succeeded.

Pretoria gasped and her hand shot to cover her mouth.

She was arrested and, as far as I know, is still serving a prison sentence, although the charge was reduced from attempted murder to malicious wounding.

I put our child into the care of Mrs Lucy Harris, now widowed, who I know to be entirely trustworthy and caring. I did this by a roundabout route to ensure the child could not be traced. Susannah is her Christian name, and she has taken the surname of Harris. Lucy has given out that she is the orphaned child of a distant relative. Susannah calls Lucy Grandma. On the few occasions she has seen me, she's called me Uncle and knows not that I am her father.

It has reached me that Lucy is not well, and I am most concerned that I am stuck over here in the Somme region in France. I have sent this letter to her so that if anything should happen to me, plans will be made for Susannah. I will not have the child returned to my wife, and she must not go to my abusive and drunken father. I don't even know if he is alive.

I know you are married and although I do not know Mr Nathaniel Moore well, I have encountered him near where I am here. I don't know whether he has told you of the circumstances in which we met, but he has proved himself to be honourable. More so than I. I have not even looked into the future enough to make provision for the child. I always thought Providence would come to my aid.

This is my final request. I beg you, for Susannah's sake, and for what might have been between us, please take my child. Tell your husband whatever you may, but take my child into safekeeping. I'm of the belief you will grow to love her, knowing she is part of me, and in the memory of what we had before I let you down so badly.

It is too late for us, but surely not for Susannah.

Pretoria, do not think harshly of me anymore. I have loved you, truly.

Simon Rashbrooke

The letter fell to her lap. Pretoria sat without a word for many minutes. Surely she could not refuse this last request from a man she had once loved to distraction. He had cared for her in his way, and the last traces of bitterness about his apparently casual treatment of her evaporated. She could think of him without quite so much pain and with only a wistful sadness.

Pretoria came back to the present when Lucy Harris made a small rasping sound in her throat.

"I assume you know the gist of the information in this letter." She picked it up and waved it.

"Yes, ma'am."

"And about his wife?"

Lucy sat forwards. "'Tis true she were in prison and maybe still is, for all I know. She 'ad a temper, true. Maybe she were driven to it. 'E were no angel but we're all products of our upbringing, I say, and I loved 'im in spite, ma'am. There were a good side to 'im, and that letter there is the witness of that."

"I didn't know much of his background," Pretoria said. "He didn't tell me."

"'E wouldn't 'ave done, yet most who met 'im liked what they saw, despite what 'e endured before. Everyone 'cept 'is father, that is, 'specially after 'is mother passed away. Poor little mite 'e was then." This was the most the woman had uttered, and it seemed to take the strength from her, for she sank back onto the cushions again. She rummaged in a little cloth bag she carried over her arm, produced a large handkerchief, and wiped her face. "Do excuse me, ma'am." She took a deep breath. "Do you want me to tell you about 'im? In 'is letter to me along of that 'un, he told me to tell if you wanted me to."

"Yes. Please do." Pretoria spoke quietly. "But please let me get us some tea first." Without waiting for a response, she left to ask Cook.

When she returned, Lucy Harris opened her eyes and started to speak. "Well, 'e is gone now, so nothing can 'urt 'im, God rest 'is soul. 'Tis only the little girl who matters now." She paused. "I was 'is nurse, you see, and looked after 'im from the start because 'is mother died 'aving 'im. Lovely girl, she were. 'Is father loved her to distraction, so 'e did. Such a gentle nature. Fair 'air and the bluest eyes, she 'ad. 'E had those eyes, didn't 'e? You'll 'ave seen that, ma'am. Those eyes! They follow the family line." She went into a reverie again.

"Perhaps that's why his father couldn't take to him," Pretoria said with sudden understanding. "Perhaps those eyes were too much of a reminder of his dead love."

"Mebbe." Mrs Harris nodded. "Aye, that was it, indeed. 'E certainly couldn't stand the sight of the little mite."

The tea arrived and Lucy paused in the telling while Cook poured, and then left them.

"Adored every pore of 'er body, 'e did." She nodded in solemn recollection. "When she died 'e locked 'imself in 'is room, 'e did, and we could 'ear 'im pacing. Wouldn't eat nothin' but drank 'imself silly every night. Kept shoutin' for more, 'e did. Ragin' an' all." She took a slurp of tea and rested.

"Poor man," Pretoria said.

"Yes, well, I was sorry for 'im at the start, but not after, with what 'e did to the boy. I 'ad to 'ide the lad away at times, 'till 'is father was sobered up enough. It went on and on, it did. 'E'd call for the boy when 'e was just a toddler, and then not remember why, it seemed. Then 'e'd shout at 'im for gettin' in the way and lash out with 'is fists, even."

"That's appalling."

"I was lucky with my own man. We took the lad in, at the end. I don't think the old man even missed 'im." She stopped, and Pretoria could hear her rasping breaths. After a rest, she said, "'E left 'ome at fifteen. Never saw 'im for a couple of years, though he wrote sometimes. I went to live with my sister when my man died."

"It's such a sad story. They could have been a comfort for each other, Simon and his father." Pretoria found her own handkerchief and blew her nose. "Then Simon found his wife," she prompted.

"Yes, ma'am. I only saw 'er a time or two. Tall, she is. Statuesque, you might say. Not pretty as such, but she 'as something about 'er. Older than 'im, she is, and she could 'ave 'ad others, I did 'ear, but when she set eyes on our boy it was 'im she wanted. And it was 'im she got."

"I think the letter has told me most of the rest," Pretoria said.

"Yes, well, 'e knew where I'd gone to, of course. 'E sort of kept in touch, now and again, like I say, but she never. Then when she did … well, what she did, 'e brought the little one to me. Then my sister passed, so it's just me and Susannah."

"How old is she now?"

"She'll be four in December." Lucy looked directly at Pretoria. "Born six months after they married, and 'im only a boy, doin' any work 'e could get. Then, more recently 'e told me 'e spent time with some posh old woman who kept 'im in riches. 'E never told me no lies or 'id the foolish things 'e got up to. Last I 'eard he met you. I believe 'e loved you. Then 'e went off to war."

"Where is the child now?"

"Left 'er with me neighbour. She's a good enough sort, but 'er 'usband 'ad the consumption and she 'as six of 'er own. Our little Susannah deserves better."

"I see."

"I daresay I could find someone to care for 'er, rather than 'er going to the Foundlin' 'Ome or the Work'ouse, but I've come because as you see, this was my Simon's last wish, ma'am."

The mute appeal in the look she gave tore at Pretoria's emotions more than anything that had been said so far. She sat with a great weight pressing upon her. This was an impossible situation.

"Mrs Harris, my husband is serving abroad, too. I … I cannot make a decision of such importance in this moment. I must think what is best to do."

"I understand, ma'am, I do, but I don't 'ave much time, see. I would 'ave come sooner, but the journey was more than I could bear for a while, and it has been sore difficult now, but I'm that worried."

"To be honest, my husband did not like Mr Rashbrooke very much." She looked away in embarrassment. "For me to take his child as a ward, well…"

"I can understand why that might be. And you, ma'am — could you love the little girl? That's what she needs more than money, a good lovin' 'ome. What will become of 'er after I'm gone? That's the thing." There was a note of pleading in the old woman's tone.

"I should like to help, Mrs Harris," Pretoria said, and then in a more resolute manner she added, "I shall write to my husband. As soon as I have a reply, I shall get in touch, I promise."

All impetus Lucy Harris might have had now seeped away, and she slumped back. She closed her eyes and two tears slid silently down her cheeks. She retrieved her handkerchief once more and dabbed at her face. "So sorry, ma'am. I understand," she whispered. "I do."

"Where are you staying tonight? It's a long return journey for you all the way to Norfolk."

Pretoria thought she muttered something about the train and an overnight stop in Peterborough.

"Come with me to the kitchen and Cook will find you some food."

The woman made to rise, but as she did so, she gave an odd rasping choke and clutched her chest, falling back heavily against the seat from which she had just struggled to get up. Her lips were blue and short breaths hissed alarmingly through her teeth, before she cried out in evident pain and fear.

Pretoria took one startled look at her and called out, "Elise! Elise! Someone, come quickly. Help us!"

Elise arrived with speed, and Pretoria's relief was immense.

"What should I do?" Panic raised the pitch of her voice.

"It looks like a heart attack," Elise said as she loosened the old woman's clothing. "Fetch some brandy and get Albert from the stables. Bring a chair. We can carry her in that, should we need to. Perhaps to a bedroom for rest."

"Shall I send someone for the doctor?"

"Yes, straight away."

Elise lifted Lucy Harris's legs and laid her along the settee as Pretoria scuttled away.

CHAPTER 17

Nathaniel surveyed the raw young faces in front of him. This is what it had come down to: children fighting in a man's position. They had little experience and only short training. Things were that desperate these days. "The Ypres salient is an area of north Belgium, surrounded on three sides by a horseshoe of higher land that the Germans occupy. That's what salient means. Perhaps you know this much, perhaps not. We Allies must continue to hold the town. You couldn't fail to see, as you arrived, the whole area has taken a severe beating several times."

A boy raised his hand. "Sir, where are all the civilians? It seemed empty when we were marched up through the Lille Gate."

"Civilians were caught up in the terror. The Hun had 'Big Bertha' back in '15. She was a massive howitzer, sixteen-and-a-half-inch shells. They were so large you heard them whooshing through the air like a train in full steam. We men were billeted in the Cloth Hall back then too, but since it was almost levelled, all the locals were eventually forced to leave."

"Here, look what I got." The young man held up a huge iron key. "It was just sitting there in a door hanging mostly off its hinges. It's the key to the Cloth Hall. Just lying there, it was. What a keepsake, aye?"

One of the youngest spoke up. "Why 'ave yer got the key to the brothel if it's in ruins?"

All the others snorted and laughed at his naivety. "Not the brothel, you nincompoop. The Cloth Hall," another said. "It was the most important building for miles around. This key could be six hundred years old."

"Wow, that's some souvenir, that is," said a third.

The exchange brought a moment of levity, and they all overreacted with their mirth. Still, it did them good.

Nathaniel continued, "These deep cellars, tunnels, and passageways in the ramparts surrounding the city were built two hundred years ago, but they shelter British troops now. Civilians had nowhere to go, so most have left."

"It's a bit of luck, if they can provide us with accommodation, medical dressing stations, and a headquarters," a slightly older man said.

Two days later Nathaniel's Company had arrived in their trench. A thick mist had come down in the night. When Nathaniel roused his troops ready for the action planned at four in the morning, the enemy trenches were completely hidden from the artillery, severely impeding the operation. He updated his superior officer at four-thirty, and at five the bombardment finally started. By the time this ended, it was too light to move forward as intended. The return fire did nothing to give him confidence of success, and he was highly relieved to be stood down until the evening. This was life. Screwing oneself up for action and then it was all cancelled.

After standing on the fire step for the best part of two hours in total, all the men were more than pleased to see the SRD coming. Nathaniel knew this stood for Supply Reserve Depot, but the men called it Service Rum Diluted or Seldom Reached Destination. Whatever it was called, they were all relieved to have a tot of rum from the stone jar. It was chilly in the early morning mist and to stand for such a long time on lookout, with sniper fire and the ground shaking with the deafening crump of shells, was taxing on the nerves.

Under cover of dusk, and following a further bombardment, hopefully the mission would be more likely to succeed. Nathaniel hoped no stray shells would blow them all to pieces before that. The enemy seemed to be concentrating on another Company to his left.

Nathaniel's nerves, along with those of his own Company of men, were pulled tight, having built themselves up for going over the top. The sun burned through the mist and beat down upon his steel helmet. It was going to be as uncomfortable as when it rained. Since all his equipment had already been cleaned and readied, he sat in the bottom of the trench with his back to the muddied sandbag wall. He was left with little else to do but think of home.

What would Pretoria be doing now? He imagined her in a pretty cotton dress with the wind in her hair. He most liked to imagine her after she had been for a ride on her horse, with strands of hair coming free, her cheeks flushed from the exercise. His stomach and chest ached. He needed his arm around her slim waist; he wanted her smile to light her eyes when she looked at him. Had he extinguished that with his stupid talk of duty? She must have believed him.

His thoughts were interrupted.

A runner arrived, hot and breathless, and threw himself down beside Nathaniel. "Message, sir, from 2nd Lieutenant Richards." This was from the Company to his left: *Have taken over Company, after officer down. Trench blown in many places. Heavy casualties. Men in splendid fettle.*

Nathaniel doubted the last sentence, but what else could the man have written, and what choice did they have but to put bravado before truth? *That could have been us*, he thought.

He scribbled a note for the young lad to take back with him and wished his compatriots good luck.

This young lad's work was not a job Nathaniel would have wanted, but he knew these runners were the most reliable method of passing messages. Corporals who did this job needed stamina and fitness. They had to be tough, and resourceful, and agile enough to leap and dodge around obstacles at speed. Running a mile in a trench that zig-zagged might mean he had only covered three hundred yards as the crow flies. It was a thankless task in many ways, but crucial.

He knew the younger brother of Pretoria's childhood friends, the Strong sisters, had run away to join the army when he was too young, having given a false age. When Nathaniel had bumped into Pretoria's brother Michael Redfern a few months back, he'd said he'd met young Hector Strong but didn't rate his chances as a runner. Then he'd heard he'd been killed, as predicted, at not quite eighteen. It was all so senseless.

Images of his wife resurged with force, and he was back on the treadmill of his thoughts. She had provided the son he'd craved, but under no circumstances had he wished her to see it as a duty, and he chided himself for suggesting that to her before they'd married. How supercilious and haughty he must have been in his proposal to her. How ridiculously patronising, yet that was not how he'd meant it at all. It had come out all wrong, because he'd been so desperate to have her by his side. He had watched her for months and months as she'd flirted and pranced and gambolled with that wretched man, Simon. Nathaniel had waited and nurtured his self-control. Then when the chance had arisen, the words he'd used had been wholly wrong. He wanted her to love him as he loved her: desperately, exclusively, and wholeheartedly.

His thoughts were interrupted again as unimaginable horror descended.

"Gas! Gas!" The cry was given to the left, and it reverberated down the line.

Nathaniel climbed a ladder and peered with care over the top of the trench. A great greenish-yellow wall of the deadly cloud was creeping across the mud towards the trench system that had received the bludgeoning from the enemy's artillery. No more than fifteen feet in depth, the gas gave off a sinister sizzling as it rolled. Nathaniel guessed that the bombardment was intended to keep the men down before this next onslaught. The gas would roll across the plain from the higher ground across the salient and seep down upon them in their holes, where they would run to shelter, believing, falsely, that was the safest thing to do.

From his position he could smell it, but it would miss his Company. Still, he shouted to his men, "Put your pads on. Hurry, put them on." They scrabbled in their kits to find the cotton-waste pad-respirators and goggles they had been issued. *Thank the lord this isn't it for us*, Nathaniel thought. *These are almost utterly useless.*

The Germans emerged over the tops of their trenches as a mass of ants, following the cloud and ready to slice the victims to finish them off, as if the burning horrors of the gas wouldn't be enough. The enemy gasmasks made the men look like demon aliens, but Nathaniel guessed they were significantly more effective than their own.

"Give it to them!" he shouted, and they each fired fifteen rounds per minute. Over and over the crack of rifles resounded at the mass of humanity ahead, and to one side as it advanced on the poor souls already suffering. Perhaps they would be glad of a German bayonet, but still he urged his own men on. Then, without warning, the enemy retreated back to their own trenches and Nathaniel's men gave cries of victory. It was a small success, and temporary, but it lifted their spirits.

Nathaniel had lived through the day and now he and his men were in the rear guard again.

He had checked on his men and written up his notes. Now, under cover of darkness, it was the safest time for moving about the city. The spotter planes of the enemy would be grounded, and the city came alive with all those thousands of men who were burrowing like insects during the day, changing positions. Some would be marching in from the south. Others might be leaving and travelling to the east through the Menin Gate and on up the Menin Road. He paused to give a thought to the poor bastards who would find themselves at Hellfire Corner when it all kicked off again. It was such a vulnerable spot, with the railway crossing the supply lines. At this moment, though, Nathaniel had some respite. He would write to Pretoria later and tell her what he could of his days, although he didn't want to upset her with the detail. He'd probably never tell of the hundreds that lay in ditches and trenches after the gas had passed. It was hard to get rid of the writhing images in his head.

What would she be doing now? He knew something of her daily routine with the estate manager and with his child. But what about the rest of the time? Had she met someone else who would not expect duty of her? He would go mad if he thought too much of that. She was young and vibrant. She deserved life at its fullest. Oh, what had he done, tying her down as he had?

He walked towards the café with several others before him. He was behind the lines now, for his rest period, and had made his way to the small town of Poperinge. He knew there was safety there, a brief respite from the terror. As he walked, his shoulder knocked into someone else.

"Here, watch it," the someone said.

Nathaniel looked up into the eyes of his brother-in-law, Michael.

"What are the odds?" Michael reached out to shake his hand.

"I knew you were moved from the Somme, but this seems to be the main theatre now in Europe."

"Have you time for a beer? I was on my way home, well, the billet, you know." Michael gave a charming smile. "Not quite home, is it?"

Nathaniel was anguished enough to forego the meal he had thought of for so long in his desperation to hear any snippet of news. "Let's go," he said.

"Shall we just go to Toc H? We can get some Flanders nectar there, forget everything for a while and have a laugh reading *The Wipers Times*."

"Yes, great idea. I'm not in the mood for the usual debauchery that goes on everywhere else."

"Me neither."

Nathaniel couldn't wait until they arrived at Talbot House, or Toc H. "What news have you of your family?" he asked.

"Probably less than you. Mother is still ruling everyone at the department store, including Father. Pretoria seems well, and I gather your property is flourishing under her care. You must be proud."

"Yes."

They arrived at the House in Rue de l'Hôpital. Its double entrance doors, with their ornate patterning in the Flemish style, stood open and welcoming to all ranks, no matter what their faith, despite having been founded by Neville, son of the Bishop of Winchester in memory of his younger brother. No soldier entering could fail to be impressed by the calm in the upstairs rooms converted from the hop-drying loft to a chapel.

Nathaniel glanced at the sign by the door: *All rank abandon, ye who enter here.* He gave a wry smile.

Once they were seated, Michael said, "I hear from Rose quite regularly, and Delphi sometimes, although she's busy doing her Women's Legion work. Rose writes in great detail. Reading her descriptions of the countryside at home is like looking at one of her paintings. Refreshing … and clean."

Nathaniel lifted his beer and looked at the light as it shone through the nectar-coloured liquid. Then, without looking at Michael, he said, "I'm not sure how things are between Pretoria and me, to be honest." Then he thought he shouldn't have said anything, but it was a relief to speak to someone who knew her.

"Oh?" Michael didn't question further so Nathaniel, having started, carried on.

"I said something thoughtless and stupid. She reacted to it as was appropriate, she thought. I've tried to show her I, well…" He found it difficult to say the word. "I … well, I love her, but she doesn't see it."

"It's impossible stuck over here. She has a good sense of what's right, though. She won't let you down and when you see her again, you can have it out. When she thinks about whatever it was, she'll realise you, of all people, wouldn't have meant it."

Nathaniel took comfort but knew it wouldn't last.

"Hey, pass that copy of *The Wipers Times*. Let's have a bit of laugh."

"When I was here before, there was an advertisement for 'Professor Dodgits Academy' and another which read, 'For Sale, The Salient estate — complete in every detail — splendid shooting — no reasonable offer refused — delay is dangerous!"

They both laughed and took gulps of their drinks, then ordered another jug.

"Hey, look at this one. 'Move with the Times and Join our Dance Classes.' That's the headline. 'We guarantee to teach you all the newest steps. These include: The Duckboard Delight, The Rifleman's Romp, The Colonel's Crawl, and the Howitzer Hop.'"

By the time they were on their third jug of the comforting beer, all poems, articles and libellous advertisements were excruciatingly funny. As they stood to leave, Michael wobbled against the table.

They staggered outside, supporting each other. The sound of shells could still be heard, but was muffled by beer and distance.

CHAPTER 18

After summoning all who might help with Lucy Harris, Pretoria stood in the hall, directing the frantic activity in order to overcome her helplessness. She sent Cook to administer the brandy, and the stable lad to fetch a stout wooden chair on which the elderly lady could be carried. She had asked Peter Goodwin to help with this task and she had sent the scullery girl to fetch the doctor.

The two men carried Lucy Harris past her on the chair. The old lady lay tipped back, with her eyes closed, a deep frown, and her skin pale and glistening.

Cook nipped around her and said she was fetching an India-rubber warming bottle. "Elise and I'll get the old lady undressed and into bed," she said over her shoulder.

Pretoria looked down at her hands, which still held Simon's letter. She headed for the morning room while all was settled upstairs. As she stood by the table, she smoothed out the paper and re-read Simon's explanation and request. Then she heaved a great sigh and carefully folded it, placing it in her pocket. *If only Nathaniel was here*, she thought. *He would know what best to do.* But then she hesitated. *What would Nathaniel say about taking Simon Rashbrooke's daughter and bringing her up as his own?*

Their last days together as husband and wife had been tense and unnatural. He had met Julia again. Perhaps her beauty and poise had tempted him once more, especially as she, Pretoria, had been heavy with child and then so ill after giving birth. Julia was free, too, by all accounts, and a known flirt. How could he resist such a temptation? Her shrewd notion was that he would not wish to take in Simon's child. He disliked the man intensely. Despite rescuing him, he had called him a worthless wretch. Well, it was true, but that wasn't the child's fault.

Everyone thought Simon had treated her shamefully, and he had, but now she knew he was a product of desperate unhappiness. If she disclosed all that she had read about his miserable childhood, his quixotic marriage, and his wife's circumstances following her crime, the world would judge him and make assumptions about his child. Of this she was sure. The judgements of society could be harsh and extraordinarily lacking in human compassion. The child would be seen as the product of a scoundrel and an attempted murderess. The little one needed protection. Pretoria could understand and forgive, but what of others?

She could not expect it of Nathaniel. It was a huge thing to ask, but she would not forgive him if he looked at the child and saw only the shortcomings of her mother and father. Yet he was an honourable man. A man who would not form an opinion like that, surely.

With an overwhelming rush, she understood at last what her husband had come to mean to her. *I love him*, she thought. *I love him with a greater strength than I ever loved Simon. Nathaniel is the centre of my being. He is my hope and my joy, and it is upon him and his safety that I depend for my own peace, my comfort and guidance, my future delight in this world.* Then her shoulders sagged. *He does not love me, but he is a man of pride, who needed me to provide an heir. I am his wife now and the mother of his son. If I accept this child, she cannot come between us.*

Again, she lurched from one thought to the next. He did not love her. Not as she needed to be loved, with tenderness and passion, in her entirety. He liked her. He probably thought her pretty enough, and what was it he had said in the park that afternoon…? Something played on the edge of her brain. He quoted three reasons for marrying her. The first and second were not particularly romantic: it was to be an arrangement where they both gained something from it. What was the third reason? Oh yes, an heir and… She shook her head, not remembering fully.

The voice at the back of her mind said Nathaniel had a right to know the truth about the little girl, Susannah, but the more she thought about it, the more apprehensive she became. Susannah would be a constant reminder to him of his rival, even though that was no longer the case.

Pretoria looked out of the window at the raindrops rolling down the glass. She wanted to weep with frustration and longing for her husband.

Yet in his absence, perhaps she could make this work. There was another way. She could concoct some story. She was certain that Lucy Harris would agree to anything, if only she would take the child. It was rash, but had she ever turned from something risky?

Elise knew her so well. Pretoria didn't think she could be a good enough liar to hoodwink her. The story would need to be convincing. Then a memory surfaced in her brain. She gasped and looked around with guilt. Would this plan that had popped into her mind work? Surely she had remembered this snippet of news for a reason.

A rap on the door made her jump. It was Elise. "The doctor is here. I've shown him in to look at that poor old soul." She stood on the threshold. There was a pause, then she continued, "Who is this Mrs Harris? Can you not tell me? It's unlike you to keep a secret from me."

Pretoria grew hot and hoped the flush hadn't spread to her face. This was going to be difficult, as she'd suspected, and she wasn't proud of herself for deceiving Elise. "I … I cannot tell you too much yet. She has come to me about a child."

"A child! What child?" Elise looked astonished.

"A little girl, Susannah. She is in Mrs Harris's charge, who has been her nurse. I can't say more. I must share the news with Nathaniel. I'll write to him immediately. How is Mrs Harris?"

"She's very poorly indeed, I think. This journey from Norfolk has been a sore trial for her, I imagine."

Pretoria took a deep breath and ploughed in. "Elise, there is no one to care for this little girl. She is orphaned. I think we should fetch her here."

"Bring her here?" Elise's voice rose. "Now, Pretoria, what are you about? Whose child is this and what claim does she have on you?"

Pretoria was not surprised by her shrewd intuition, but she was cornered, and she resorted to unnatural aloofness. "I've already said, I need to contact Nathaniel before I say more."

Elise coloured a dull red. "I'm sure I beg your pardon if you think I have asked too much, but Mr Moore and your mother trust me to look after you in their absence."

"I'm an adult, now, and must take certain responsibilities." Then Pretoria regretted her tone. "Oh, Elise, I know and I'm sorry. It's all a lot to take in. There are some things about which only I can make decisions. Dear, dear Elise, will you please, please go to Norfolk and fetch the little girl back here? I doubt Mrs Harris will be well enough to travel for some time, and meanwhile the child is in the most unsatisfactory conditions, I understand. We can decide about her future once she is here. Don't be angry with me."

"Very well." Elise was still stiff in her manner.

"Just until Mrs Harris is better," Pretoria repeated.

"If she gets better," Elise said. "I believe her heart must be in a very poor state."

"I'll organise for you to be taken to the station in the trap. I think you will need an overnight stay. It will be quite a journey. Would you like Peter to accompany you? I'm sure the estate can do without him for a couple of days."

"It might be best. I'm not that well versed with trains and the like, not on my own," Elise said.

"Will you ask the doctor to come to me here in the morning room as soon as he is finished?"

"I'll go up now." Elise turned.

As she left the room, Pretoria let out a deep breath. She had got through the first part of her deception, although she wished the floor could swallow her. She hated lying to Elise.

When the doctor arrived, she realised this was only the beginning as her fears were confirmed. "She cannot last more than a few days, I fear, Mrs Moore," he said. "Her heart is in a shocking condition. If she has relatives, I advise you to contact them with all speed."

"She has no one, apparently. She is a widow and has no children of her own. There is only a little girl, who she looks after, and Elise will travel to fetch her here tomorrow."

"I really don't think your visitor should have undertaken the journey here. From Norfolk, I gather. Who is she?"

"She is the nurse of an old friend of mine." The story had started. The lie was beginning. "Thank you, doctor. I'll see you out."

When Pretoria went upstairs, she was shocked at the sight of the old lady. Her face looked sunken and grey, and her breaths came in shallow gasps. Cook was sitting next to the bed. Pretoria thanked her and she stood and left the room.

"Mrs Harris," Pretoria whispered, "it's Pretoria Moore." The woman's eyelids flickered. "It's Simon's friend, Pretoria, Mrs Harris. You came to see me. Do you remember?"

Recognition dawned slowly across her face and Mrs Harris opened her slack lips to mutter something. Her expression grew anxious. "Sus-Susannah," she whispered and Pretoria leaned closer, taking the elderly lady's hand.

"Susannah will be cared for. We shall fetch her here. We will look after everything. Don't be afraid." Pretoria stroked the old lady's brow and her expression eased.

Mrs Harris gave the ghost of a nod before her eyes closed once more. "God bless you," she muttered but could manage no more.

As the old woman slept, Pretoria crept from the room. She must write to her husband.

July 1917

My dearest Nathaniel,

Our little Arthur continues to thrive, although he does cry a lot. I think he picks up on my own uncertainties about what is best for him, but I am learning all the time and of course Elise is here to help me.

We have heard that our Michael is coming home. He has been injured by the horrendous gas we hear about, but he is alive. Rose will be so relieved. I believe they have come to an understanding, and so I'm sure there will be a marriage as soon as he is well enough. Mama and Mrs Strong, as well as our fathers, will be rejoicing. It seems so awful to be pleased that he is injured, but it means he is able to come home. He may need further treatment once he has returned.

May we be reunited soon, too, but not if you must be wounded in order for that to happen. Please be careful.

My next news is very strange. You probably never knew my particularly good friend, Maud Lawson. She married a Mr Hatch, and they went to live in India as neither of them had any family left to stay here with. We grew extremely close. As close as sisters, almost, while we were growing up.

That was the first part of the pretence. They had been more like acquaintances, really.

When I had a visit from Margaret Parks after Arthur was born, among other things, she told me of the tragic death of both Maud and her husband. I'm not sure I shared that before. My mind was on other things which she told me, at the time, and on our little Arthur.

Well, the strangest thing has happened. They left a child. A little girl called Susannah, and of course, she has no other living relatives and travelled back to England with her nurse, Mrs Harris.

Mrs Harris came to visit me here because Maud and I were so friendly.

The lie was set. Pretoria explained all that had happened with Mrs Harris and how Elise had gone to fetch Susannah. That last part was all true.

As Pretoria sat thinking, she nibbled on the end of her pen before dipping it in the ink again. This was all so troubling. She could, and did, speak truthfully about the plight of the little one if she was not given a home with them. Then she pondered again about the names. It wouldn't be so strange if the little girl referred to herself as Harris instead of Hatch. The names were similar, and for several months she had been cared for by the old woman who had, in fact, given her own name to protect Susannah from her irrational and dangerous mother. No one need know that.

She finished her letter with a little pleading to her husband for his sympathy and understanding, told him of the latest on the estate and that the calving appeared to be going well, and signed herself a loving and dutiful wife.

The following morning, Elise was ready to make her long journey to Norfolk to fetch Susannah.

"Please, take this letter. It's for the woman who is looking after the little one and explains everything. There's a little money to cover expenses while she has cared for the child, too. Susannah is certain to be frightened and bewildered." Pretoria sighed. "You will comfort her, won't you? Of course, I know you will, dearest Elise, it's what you are best at."

"That I will. You can rely on me for all of that. Whoever she is, she is but a mite and will need kindness. I couldn't refuse that to any child in need."

Pretoria waved her and Peter off with relief. So far, everything was working. With guilt she thought about Lucy Harris and Nathaniel. At least he would be unable to question Elise about the child's background. Only she knew the truth, and Simon's last letter was hidden away at the back of one of her drawers.

Her self-condemnation for the fiction was immense. She loved Nathaniel and she vowed to explain all properly, face to face. It would be impossible by letter and with such a distance between them. She sent up a silent prayer for his safety.

CHAPTER 19

Nathaniel opened the letter from Pretoria. Before he read any of it, he looked down at the salutation. This had assumed huge significance for him in his enforced absence. He was due back in the forward trenches on the next evening and he needed, with all the utter desperation of his being, to know that she loved him. There it was. That word. That single condemnation — 'dutiful'. *Your dutiful and loving wife*, she wrote. He put his elbows on his knees and his head down on his hands for several long moments.

After he'd taken a deep breath, he read the story of Mrs Harris and the child Susannah. This was typical of Pretoria. She was so soft-hearted and would take in any waif if she heard such a story. He was moved by it himself. He folded the letter carefully.

The last day's rest was largely spent sleeping and preparing his mind for the next onslaught, but he wrote to Pretoria first.

July 7ᵗʰ, 1917
My Dearest Wife,

I've been here so long I can't bear it, but I must. After so many battles, with small amounts of ground gained and lost again, they are suggesting this next will be the most successful. Haven't we heard that all before? When the tunnellers blew mines and we took the Messines Ridge, it all seemed promising. I remember that set of blasts. Nineteen in total, there were, and lumps of blue clay as big as houses flying through the air which left one of the craters one hundred yards across. I remember the whole hillside rocked like a ship on the ocean and the thunder was deafening. Yet still the Germans retook any ground we made.

I'm sending this in a green envelope for 'intimacy', and you'll note the absence of blue censorship pencil, for I've been responsible for that since my latest promotion. Still, I shall be patriotic and give away nothing of value to the enemy. However, I can translate the order generously!

With all the months of shelling, the complicated drainage system in the salient is wrecked. The land is covered in mud. It is not ordinary mud. It sticks to us and slows us down. Men's boots and putties are solid with it anyway, but it's like porridge and covers the bottoms of our trousers. All the duckboards that snake across the land are covered in it, and very slippery. If you fall off those, you've had it. It's so deep it can suck a tank into it, never mind a man.

When I first came to this town, the Germans on the ridge were hidden among the trees. In fact, one of our guys saved himself from the gas, which creeps along the ground down here, by climbing a tree. Now there are no trees anywhere. All are grey-blue stumps sticking out of the grey-blue mud.

Yet for all this dismal talk, for which I apologise, there is a pact between us men that we share each other's troubles and get each other out of danger. You wouldn't believe the compassion and brotherly love.

We have made some small gains and now we have a different man at the helm, General Plumer, so maybe, just maybe, we can take this small place, rather than attacking on a wide front, and it will make a huge difference. It's called Passchendaele.

I will write again, God willing.

Love from

Your Nathaniel

As Pretoria read Nathaniel's latest letter yet again, her desperation was palpable. His morale sounded lower than she had ever known it. All she wanted was to enfold him in her arms, wipe his memory clean, kiss away his thoughts. He hadn't mentioned her plan to accept Susannah as her ward. Perhaps their letters had crossed.

If he was killed on this next offensive, she would never forgive herself for her deception. In her mind, superstition took hold. If he was spared once more, she would tell him everything. *Please God, let me see him again, whole and safe.*

Two days passed and Mrs Lucy Harris slipped away from the world, in peace at last, leaving Pretoria with her story to tell Elise, and then the rest of her acquaintances. The doctor arranged for a woman in the town to come to prepare her. As soon as the grave was dug, there was a short ceremony in the local graveyard, with Pretoria, Cook, and the doctor attending.

Later that day a message came via a boy on a horse, from the home of her parents. Tamsin had gone missing, and Gisela with her.

Missing? My sister is missing? What silly mischief has she got into now? Thought Pretoria as she paced the rooms downstairs. *Oh, Nathaniel, how I need you, yet what would you make of all this turmoil? Oh Lord, perhaps it's best you are not here.* She wrung her hands.

An hour passed. Two hours. Pretoria waited with impatience for the sound of wheels on the driveway. She was consumed with curiosity about Simon's child, which drove away all thoughts of her wayward sister, who was probably playing some silly prank and would have returned by dusk.

If the child resembled Simon, then some further explaining would be necessary. For the thousandth time, she wondered if she was committing a completely foolish act. Then she heard the approaching vehicle outside.

Pretoria ran to the front door. As she opened it, she was just in time to see Elise climb down stiffly, with the help of Peter Goodwin. In her arms was a sleeping child. It had been a long journey. All she could see was the curve of an immature cheek and some tendrils of brown hair escaping from an old sunbonnet. At least the child had not inherited her father's guinea-gold locks.

"Elise, I am so pleased to see you. I have been on hot coals waiting for your return. I hope your journey hasn't been too awful. I'm so grateful." She turned to Peter. "Thanks to you, also. I don't doubt your assistance has been invaluable." She held out her arms and Elise handed her the sleeping infant. "Come in before we talk further. Peter, will you join us for some refreshment?" Pretoria whispered so as not to wake the sleeping child.

He hesitated and gave Elise a searching look. She studiously ignored it, which puzzled Pretoria. Then he said, "Thank you, ma'am, but no. I'll get myself home to my own bed. I'm pleased to have been of help."

"Thank you, Peter," Elise replied, and a smile lit her face.

Once indoors, Pretoria looked down at the child and was utterly relieved to see that she did not resemble Simon at all. The softly rounded cheeks brushed by dark lashes were almost those of a baby. The lips were full and the mouth generous. The little nose had slightly flared nostrils but was, as yet, still a button, and not yet properly formed. The child's hair was a little damp with perspiration and curled on her forehead. Surely no one would guess this was Simon's daughter. His locks, as well as being exceptionally blond, were straight and heavy. The little girl didn't have his long leanness either, but had the sturdy little body of a country child, with dimples on her knuckles where her fingers protruded from a frayed cuff.

As relief flooded Pretoria's mind, the child stirred. For a single second her lashes lifted, and the bluest speedwell eyes stared at Pretoria without recognition. Pretoria caught her breath and gulped, before the little one uttered a small shuddering sigh and, turning her face, snuggled against her, in a deep sleep once more. Anyone who had known Simon Rashbrooke would surely recognise the colour of those eyes.

She shot a glance across at Elise to see if she had witnessed her shock, but the older woman had turned to organise the fetching of the luggage from the cart. Cook came through from the back corridor and offered to take the child, but Pretoria shook her head. "She knows Elise, now. If she wakes among further strangers, she may be fearful."

When Elise returned, they both went upstairs to the nursery, where little Arthur was sleeping soundly. It was a large room with heavy green and cream curtains. The carpet, green and beige, was worn but still serviceable. The wallpaper was patterned with images of children playing and dancing, some around a corn sheaf, and others holding hands with grown-ups wearing country clothes. Each image was surrounded by a garland of pretty leaves and rosebuds. This would be a fitting room for a little girl to grow and flourish.

Arthur lay in his barred cot, since he was too long for his wicker swinging cradle. Pretoria leaned over and tucked the little silken eiderdown further around him. He grunted in his sleep and pushed it off again. She sighed. He wasn't the easiest of toddlers, but perhaps, she thought again, that reflected her own tensions.

The room was full of toys. Some must have been Nathaniel's when he was a small boy. There was the Victorian rocking horse with the fierce eyes. Pretoria wasn't keen on its stare, but Nathaniel still loved it. She was momentarily transported back to the time he had told her of the adventures he'd had on this horse, pretending to be a Viking, a Roman soldier, a cowboy in the Americas. His eyes had sparkled, and he'd given her a cheeky self-conscious grin.

The wooden playpen stayed up permanently. It was useful when Arthur was awake, now he was travelling. There was heavy oak furniture upon which Elise or Pretoria could dress him, and in the corner a box overflowed with a little wooden trainset, toy bricks and other paraphernalia. Still, despite all this, Pretoria had managed to find a space, and the stable lad had been kind enough to put up the little bed with a tented canopy, which might give the girl some security when she awoke.

Elise lay the child down and carefully began to remove her bonnet and slide her arms out of her coat. Had she made the connection with Simon? She had intimated nothing yet. Pretoria stood to one side and watched, her whole body tense. If Elise had noticed anything, she would be sure to say it in her forthright Yorkshire way. However, all she said was, "I'll get her undressed and into bed as soon as possible. She's all worn out, poor little mite. She wasn't a good traveller on the train, either. To start with she was that excited, she was bouncing about like a puppy and chattering like a sparrow, then she was sick. The adventure of strangeness, I suppose."

"Has she asked after Mrs Harris?" Pretoria asked.

"A couple of times she asked where her 'Grandma' was. I said she had to go away for a while, and I was taking her to see a pretty lady. It seemed to satisfy. She's not too shy. A friendly little soul, in fact," Elise said.

"You must be very tired and hungry too," Pretoria said. "I'll ask Cook to bring us some sandwiches on trays. We could eat in the snug and talk. The fire is roaring. You must tell me how it was when you arrived in Norfolk and what sort of place she has been living in." Once they were settled with their food, Pretoria's questions began. "Did you find the place without difficulty? What did the lady who was caring for her say, when

129

she read my letter? How was the journey? I do hope it wasn't too far from the station at the other end."

Elise finished her mouthful and said, "Hold on, lass. One at a time."

Pretoria gave a crooked smile of apology.

"The carter at the other end knew where to take us, and it wasn't far. The place was small and rundown, with only basic rough wood furniture. The curtains, what there were of them, had definitely seen better days, but the woman herself seemed kind-hearted enough. I didn't see her man, but I heard someone upstairs croaking and coughing."

"I do hope the little mite hasn't caught anything. Consumption can be contagious, but you must know more about that than I."

"I understand it's called tuberculosis now. The woman assured me her man was no longer infectious. He's been away for months in a sanatorium paid for by his employer, and the little girl has been kept away. After all, she was only there for a few days."

"We must be sure to take her clothes and burn them and watch for any signs at all."

"Yes, indeed. I bundled them up, rather than leaving them in the nursery. I'm sure there is no danger; I wouldn't have suggested we put her in there if there was. Still, if you are concerned, we need to look out for night sweats, fatigue, and wasting, but I have to say she's not wasting away at the moment. She's a stocky little thing. The other children were a ragged little bunch and not too clean. It must be difficult for that poor woman. She was a wiry, lean soul."

"Poor woman, indeed. And did you give her…?"

"I gave her the money, like you said, for looking after Susannah. 'Twas a tadge pathetic to see how grateful she was."

She took another bite. "She said Mrs Harris had been ailing for some time and was very worried for what would become of the child in the future."

"Yes, I understood that, from the brief conversation I had with the old lady before she passed away."

"All the difference in the world between that cottage and where the neighbour was looking after her from what I saw. The neighbour took me in to Mrs Harris's to gather the rest of Susannah's things." Elise took a long draught from her cup. "There's not much. The place was spotless, despite her being so poorly. The child's clothes are all darned and patched, but clean."

"We'll have to take her to Sylvie's in the town and get her sorted out with new dresses," Pretoria said.

"The neighbour said a young man came by from time to time. Blond hair, good-looking. She reckoned he paid the rent for Mrs Harris," Elise said.

Pretoria was aware of the tell-tale flush. "Oh?" She avoided Elise's gaze. "This fire is so warm," she said. "It's making me quite sleepy and overheated. You must be tired, too. Have you finished eating? I think I'd like to look in on Susannah and Arthur before I go to bed."

CHAPTER 20

Pretoria was up and about early, the morning after Susannah's arrival. She didn't even wait for her morning drink to be brought but put on her day dress and hurried up the stairs to the nursery. Elise had just finished feeding Arthur, and he was rolling around in the playpen.

He looked at her as she entered the room and gave her a toothless grin. It warmed her spirit. As a newborn, he'd cried a great deal and vomited constantly. She'd felt immensely guilty that motherhood had not brought automatic love. It had all been such hard work when she was constantly exhausted. Elise had told her that her milk was probably not rich enough for such a bonny boy, which had added another layer of self-blame. As soon as Arthur had started taking supplementary food, he'd seemed more settled. Now, he responded to her presence with these beaming smiles, and she had grown to love him more. He was part of her and part of Nathaniel; part of him that would be with her always, no matter what happened.

She leaned down and took his hand. "Hello, little one. Are you all fed and comfy? What have you got there?" She rolled a squashy, colourful ball with bells inside, and he manoeuvred himself over to watch it.

Distracted as he was, Pretoria turned her attention to the child who sat on a stool at a small wooden table. In front of her was a bowl of oatmeal porridge, which she spooned into her mouth with vigour. She wore a dress of flowered cotton and a patched pinafore, which had gone grey with many washes. Elise had found some pink ribbon, with which she had tied back the front of Susannah's hair.

"This is the lady that I said we were coming to see," Elise said. "Say 'good morning Mrs Moore'."

The child stopped eating and stared silently and unnervingly at Pretoria. Then she smiled. It lit her face, and a roguish sparkle appeared in those wide blue eyes. There was no doubt she'd inherited some of her father's charm. Pretoria swallowed. Then the girl returned to her breakfast. Pretoria took the opportunity to study the little face. Certainly, she had no look of Simon, except for her eyes. Her hair was dark and curly, and little glints of sun highlighted its fine texture. Pretoria glanced at Elise, who looked at her with one eyebrow raised in a question. Pretoria studiously ignored this.

Having scooped up all the porridge, Susannah cast a swift glance at Pretoria before she scrambled off the stool and skipped to the window, where she rested her hands on the ledge. After a brief moment, she hopped from one foot to the other, and then turned with excitement. "Look! Elise, look." She pointed. "Horses, and a baby one."

"It's not a baby, but it's very small," Pretoria said as she joined the child at the casement. Miss Hibiscus and Nathaniel's bay stallion, along with a small Shetland pony, were cropping the grass in the field behind the garden. Pretoria was forever thankful that these horses had been overlooked in the round-up following pleas for such animals to go overseas at the start of the war. She was sure Peter was responsible for that, but they avoided the subject. She appreciated his loyalty to Nathaniel and now to herself. "Do you like horses?" Pretoria looked down at the shining face.

"Uncle Simon rides a horse. He came to see us yesterday, but Grandma said he has to go away."

"It wasn't yesterday, poppet. The other day, perhaps." Pretoria knew it had been many weeks, even months ago, but time would mean nothing to this little one.

The use of Simon's name came as a shock, and she looked behind her to see if Elise had heard. Fortunately, Elise had taken the breakfast things out to the little nursery kitchen.

"When is Grandma coming back?"

More difficulty, but not as risky as what had just passed. "I can't say for certain, poppet. But this will be like a little holiday for you. Do you think you will enjoy it? Perhaps Cook will give us something for the horses to eat and we could go and feed them, later."

"Oh, yes." More hopping ensued. "Shall we go now?"

"Susannah, I don't think I heard you ask to leave the table." Elise had returned. She looked at Pretoria. "No harm in starting as we mean to proceed." She smiled and Pretoria nodded.

Susannah clambered back onto the stool and said, "Leave table, please."

After receiving Elise's nod, she slithered down again and ran back to the window, looked up at Pretoria, gave that cheeky grin, and gazed out.

"I'll take the children outside if they are finished with breakfast, then you can have a break," Pretoria said.

"I think she'll be one to need occupation. She was awake just after six and has been on the go since then. She's a lively one, with a quick mind, I think. Her manners have been generally good, though."

"Perhaps she'll have a little sleep after lunch. We'll leave you now." Pretoria picked up Arthur, and balancing him on her hip, she took the little girl's hand. They went down the two flights of stairs in search of Cook.

That afternoon, Pretoria collapsed onto a sofa in the drawing room for half an hour before the children awoke. She needed to see Peter about estate matters later. One of the tenants had fallen and badly sprained her ankle, as well as cutting her hands. Pretoria needed Peter to look at the pathway she had tripped on to see if they could arrange for the broken slabs to be replaced. She would take a parcel of food, too. Then there was the winter barley sowing to ask about, and she needed to see if the oats they'd planted last month were thriving. She had learned that cows' gestation was two hundred and eighty-three days, so she also had to ask Peter when the bull would be brought over from Burthwaite. At one time, she would not have dreamed she would be discussing things so indelicate with a man, and one who was not her husband. *Oh, Nathaniel. I do miss you*, she thought for the hundredth time.

As she sat, she idly picked up the November copy of *The Bystander*. Captain Bruce Bairnsfather was becoming quite well-known for his irreverent cartoons of life on the Front in *Fragments from France*. On the back was an advertisement for Royal Vinolia toothpaste. She smiled at the slogan, which said, 'Ready for Inspection' and the line of soldiers, each with a rifle, except for the one nearest, who had the tube of paste. Everything reflected the times. Even something as mundane as this. It reminded her of something else she had to check. Had they a toothbrush for Susannah?

Her mind shot back to the reference the child had made to Uncle Simon. Pretoria had another panic about how she would carry off this deception. She was desperate to see Nathaniel again and have his arms around her. It would be so much easier to explain everything if he were here. If only they could get past whatever it was that had held him back after Arthur's birth, during his last leave. Her longing was a physical ache.

She tried to picture him, but all she could see was a morass of mud. *Please don't let this be a premonition. I need you, my love*, she thought.

CHAPTER 21

The men picked their way across the Grote Markt. It was difficult in the dark, but a path had been swept. It was the safest time to move about because enemy aerial spotters couldn't fly and the guns on the hills were silent. As they passed the famous Cloth Hall, now almost completely wrecked, Nathaniel remembered the witty advertisement in *The Wipers Times*, which stated that the auditorium had a lifting roof and perfect ventilation. Now he looked at the skeletal ruins of the once proud and bustling building, fit only for bats and the occasional owl.

After dusk had fallen, the streets were busy with troops hurrying to their posts or scurrying about other business. The whole town was a pile of rubble and dust, but now there was a quiet and anxious expectation in the air that was almost tangible. This wasn't just another forthcoming battle, they all hoped.

The smaller battles that had been planned and executed had been deemed successful, but at huge cost to those who had lost limbs, been burned and blinded with gas, or drowned in the sucking mud. Three months ago, Nathaniel had read that General Sir Douglas Haig had said, "In my opinion, the war can only be won here in Flanders."

Here they were, still fighting, still losing men, and Nathaniel was sick of it. Sick of the futility, and sick of missing his family while he lay in the stinking morass of mud and blood, plagued by lice and doubts. It was so hard to remain positive, and he was aware that all around him morale was low. "Best foot forward, lads. Heads up and get the job done, once and for all," he shouted in grim determination.

He'd written another letter and left it back at headquarters for safekeeping. It seemed like yet another farewell, in the event of … well. Just in case. He'd told Pretoria he loved her, in spite of everything. He missed her good sense and laughter. He wanted more than anything to bury his face in her hair and inhale deeply, or to lie peacefully in her arms.

He said he understood about her wanting to take care of this child, although in his own mind he thought it a little strange that the old nursemaid had brought her the charge. He didn't say this in his letter. It was not the time when he was hundreds of miles away.

His thoughts turned to recent information imparted by his senior officer at the briefings. Allied gains had been made to the east of Ypres at Langemarck in August, even though apparently German morale was higher than expected. Since then, General Plumer's 'bite and hold' strategy along the infamous Menin Road meant that when about fifteen hundred yards were gained here, the troops would dig in while another wave would overtake them and attack further. This meant that German troops, instead of finding war-weary, disoriented soldiers, were confronted with a well organised defensive line. The strategy seemed to be working.

Now there were troops from all over the world coming to fight for King and Empire. Nathaniel heard accents from as far afield as Canada, Southern Rhodesia, Australia and the Caribbean, and General John Pershing's troops from America had added their weight to the fight seven months ago. Germany had adopted the risky strategy of sinking American ships around British waters carrying goods to the Allies. It was a policy that had backfired. *Thank God*, Nathaniel thought, *because it's brought the might of the USA in at last.*

The army for the forthcoming battle was the largest Britain had ever fielded, Nathaniel was told in the briefing the day before. The place highlighted for the coming attack, Passchendaele, was a small village up on the ridge but strategically, if they could stick the enemy there, it would be a gallant and wonderful victory, they were told.

Nathaniel tried to be optimistic after what he had heard, but it was so difficult. Yet he had to chivvy his Company into believing this was a great push and worth doing for the survival of their families back at home. Oh, how he missed his baby son, who he didn't even know, and it was becoming difficult to picture Pretoria. He still had the grainy grey photograph, but he could no longer hear her voice in his head, and it scared him.

CHAPTER 22

Again, Pretoria was up early in the morning with the birds. Listening to the dawn chorus was always a joy, although today her thoughts turned to a premonition she'd had as she'd gone to sleep. This time, it had not been about Nathaniel, but her sister.

Someone came thundering up the driveway, making such a racket on the gravel that Pretoria leapt from her seat, hurried down to the hall, and peered out of the window. A lanky lad, riding a sturdy piebald cob, swung his leg over the animal's bare back and jumped down, scattering gravel over its huge, feathered hooves. There was a loud rap on the door. Being the nearest, Pretoria opened it in haste. The messenger breathed heavily with his exertions and thrust a letter at her.

Pretoria's heart was fluttering, and immediately she feared the worst for Nathaniel. But this wasn't an official postman from the GPO, nor was the letter the right colour for a telegram. She took a deep breath. No good news came this way.

The boy said, "From Mr and Mrs Redfern, missus. Apologies for not going around to the servants' entrance, missus, but I'm to give it to you directly."

Memories of the first note swam in her mind, and her first reaction was one of immense relief that it didn't concern Nathaniel. She hadn't realised how tense she was until her neck muscles and shoulders relaxed. However, her thoughts leapt to her sister. What on earth had she got herself into now?

The note was signed by both her parents, but Pretoria could tell it was dominated by her mother's tones. Was there imperious over-exaggeration or genuine fear in the words? They described how Tamsin had left a note inside a magazine on the hall table at home. It had told of the fate of a young German boy at the hands of some rough men in the army town of Colchester. He had received severe bruises and ended up in a coma for five days, apparently. Tamsin feared for her friend, Gisela, especially since comments had been made within her hearing. She didn't specify what she had heard.

She has been excessively interested in this Women's Land Army. We fear she has taken steps to join this organisation and taken Gisela with her. Gisela's mother is distrué avec inquiétude, as are we both.

Pretoria's felt her usual exasperation at her mother's use of French, which was probably incorrect anyway. She was sure Gisela's mother was distraught, but her own parents sounded more cross than worried. Then again, Tamsin had always been wayward, and certainly not particularly concerned about her clothing or looks. Pretoria wouldn't have put it past her to have gone off and joined the Land Army. Hadn't she talked of it when she'd visited last?

However, she doubted her sister would have much idea about the work involved, no matter how well-intentioned she was in protecting her friend and wanting to do something useful in the war effort. But she would never have been content to knit socks or put together food parcels for their men at the front. She would want something far more dramatic and, in her eyes, romantic. As for Gisela, she was almost as bad.

Pretoria was frustrated with her sister, although there was a little worm of worry, too. She didn't need this right now, but clearly her parents wanted her to do something.

"Thank you for this." She addressed the boy. "Go around to the kitchen door and I'll ask Cook to give you some sustenance for your trouble. Then before you return, I'll give you a letter to take back to Mr and Mrs Redfern."

The boy gave a cheeky grin, touched his forehead with two fingers in a salute of sorts, and with the exuberance of the young and with the thought of food, he found more energy, bounded down the steps, and loped around the corner of the house.

Pretoria beat him to the kitchen to speak with Cook, then took herself off to write a hurried note. She considered asking Peter to go to see her parents, but he'd only just returned from one errand of importance for her, and it didn't seem right to ask him to go on another.

In the end, she decided to take Miss Hibiscus and go to see her parents herself. Her horse was fit and young. Much of the journey would be along lanes where she could trot, and across fields where she could probably up her pace, which would be good. It would take her two or three hours to do the fifteen miles or so, but she would be there by late lunchtime if she hurried. At least she would hear the truth of things and find out for herself what steps had already been taken. She could stay the night, which would be necessary for her horse, as well as herself, and return tomorrow.

It took half an hour to prepare for the journey, speak to Elise, and see Cook, who gave her a packet of hurriedly put together sandwiches and an apple.

The day was cool but dry, and she made good time. Mama was pleased to see her, and fat tears rolled down her cheeks. "Let me show you what she wrote." She hurried from the room, returning with the magazine and the note. "She reads too many trashy novels. As for Gisela, how could she have allowed Tamsin to design such a plan?"

"Have you spoken to Izzy Strong or her mother?"

"No. I'm not sure I wish to share this disgrace with any of our friends. Whatever will they think?"

Pretoria sighed. "If you want to find her, then that is what must be done. Where is Papa?"

"He's had to go to the store. Some staff crisis. As if this isn't a crisis! He assumes she'll return when she sees how hard it is to find work."

Pretoria guided her mother to a seat.

"Everyone knows that farmers resist having female workers on their land, which is ridiculous, since women have supported the work of their men since time began. When she talked of this Land Army, I said to her, 'Utter nonsense. Under no circumstances will a child of mine do such a thing.' Prejudice, that's what that is. Women are perfectly capable of milking a cow, and how many women help their men at harvest, or with butter-making? 'The Lilac Sunbonnet Brigade', they were called in '15. How insulting is that? But it's not a thing for *my* daughter to contemplate. Her work at the store is important, surely. And another thing…"

"Mama!" Pretoria didn't have time for all this. "I shall go to see Mrs Strong and ask Izzy what she knows. Those three share all their secrets and dreams."

"Preti, my dear. Do come in," Mrs Strong said. "It's a while since we met. You look well, but a little tired, if I may say. Most of the family are out, although I think Izzy is upstairs."

"I'm so sorry to disturb you unannounced like this."

"I hadn't realised you were back at home. To visit, I imagine? All is well, is it not?" Mrs Strong looked anxious. Such was the lot of women left at home. " It's a miracle that Michael is home. Your mother must be so relieved, and it's happy news that he and Rose are to be married. Such a joy."

"Indeed. We're all delighted, but we worry about his continuing ill health. Because of this awful gas, his lungs are still not mended," Pretoria said.

"Rose tells me he has gone to a sanatorium by the sea to complete his recuperation. Rhyl in North Wales, she said, which isn't too far away, I suppose."

"Yes. Such a conflict of emotions. We look forward to a wedding when he is recovered enough." Pretoria smiled. "That will cheer us all, but maybe not for a few months yet. I wondered if I might have a word with Izzy."

"Yes, of course. Is there a problem in that quarter? I only ask, because now I see you are in a hurry and a little out of sorts."

"It concerns Tamsin and the daughter of Frau Schröder."

"Gisela? Have they been up to mischief again? Oh dear! Izzy has not set foot from the house these last few days, and she has not had a German lesson in over two weeks. Some of the local people have been really quite nasty about our German friend. Some of the words they used are truly upsetting."

"I'm so sorry to hear that, Mrs Strong. Both the mother and daughter are lovely people, but some can speak cruelly when they are frightened about something else altogether."

"Excuse me while I call Izzy." She left the room and Pretoria heard her call. When she returned, and while they waited for Izzy, Mrs Strong said, "You have grown up, Pretoria. Last time we spoke, you seemed almost a child. Now you are a beautiful woman, with *two* children, I hear?"

"Yes, the daughter of an old friend, newly orphaned, has come to stay with us for a while." She was deliberately vague.

Mrs Strong might well remember Maud Hatch. However, if she were to promulgate the story she had invented, now might be the time to test it. She took a deep breath. "You might remember Maud Lawson, who married a Mr Hatch. Susannah is their child."

"Mmm. Vaguely. I heard they had a child and were killed in a carriage accident out in India. Such a tragedy. But I thought…"

At that moment Izzy came into the room, rescuing Pretoria from further explanation. She was a tall child, slim, with the same flyaway hair as her oldest sister, Rose. She had no need to wear glasses, though. She had not yet blossomed into the unmistakeable mature beauty of her middle sister, Delphi, but she was pretty and possessed calm intelligence in her expression. She nodded and said, "Good day Preti."

Pretoria couldn't help but wonder if there was a guarded expression in her eyes.

"Izzy, Pretoria would like to speak to you about Tamsin. Sit down, child."

Izzy took the little salon chair so that both the older ladies could see her clearly from their place beside each other, on the settee.

"Izzy, please don't be alarmed. I'm sure you are not involved in my family's predicament. It's just that we cannot find Tamsin, and Gisela seems to have gone missing, too."

"Oh, my goodness!" Mrs Strong exclaimed as one hand covered her mouth and the other shot to her bosom. "Izzy, you must tell all that you know, straight away." Izzy hesitated. "Iris, come along, child. I can see you know something. What's going on?" Mrs Strong, despite her tired and often feeble demeanour since the death of her youngest son, sounded firm in this request.

Izzy cleared her throat, looked sideways, and then sat up straighter. She realised there was no escape. "We were in town the other day and there was a poster in the shop window. We could hardly miss it. It was large and bright yellow."

"Yes, yes, but what's it got to do with Tamsin?" Mrs Strong said.

"I'm trying to say," Izzy said with a little streak of determination. "It said, 'Get Behind the Girl He Left Behind. Join the Land Army'. There was a picture of a girl in work clothes and an outline of a soldier in uniform, behind."

Pretoria nodded. "And Tamsin was interested in this?"

"She's been talking about it for a while, but then outside church a couple of weeks ago, some of the girls were being really horrid to Gisela and calling her the most awful unpatriotic names. I can't tell you the words. They were too cruel." Izzy looked down at her fingers as they picked at a thread in her skirt.

"I understand from Frau Schröder that things have been difficult," Mrs Strong said. "Leave that thread, Izzy, you'll make a hole."

"The man in the shop said they pay eighteen shillings. That's a lot of money. He said he had a leaflet that someone from the … what was it? The Women's National Land … Service, that was it. Anyway, this person visited and left the leaflets, so Tamsin and Gisela both took one, but I didn't." The girl looked worried. "I didn't want to be unpatriotic, but … well, with Hector, um, well … gone and Delphi away, I couldn't leave you and Papa." She looked at her mother with troubled eyes.

Pretoria leaned forward. "Did the girls say where they might have gone to join this Land Army, Izzy?"

"No. I don't know anything else. I would say if I did, honestly, I would." Tears glittered, but she managed to control them, taking a gulp of air.

"That's alright, Izzy. Thank you for telling us this much," Pretoria said.

"You should have said straight away, Iris!"

Pretoria stood. "I better get back to Mama, to tell her and Papa all that you have told me. Thank you, Mrs Strong, Izzy."

Before returning home, Pretoria spent the next twenty minutes riding into town to find a copy of the leaflet that Tamsin had taken. Perhaps it would have a contact address, and at least she could leave her parents' home knowing she had done all that was possible.

Pretoria's letter to Nathaniel, once she was at home again, detailed all that had happened, but it sounded empty. It was becoming more difficult to write because everything had a delay, as if she spoke with an echo that sent her own words skittering back to her. She wanted to face him and speak with all her heart. Tears threatened to spill, and she looked up to dispel them. Then she sealed and addressed the envelope knowing he wouldn't receive it for days, and by then everything would have moved forward and be different. For all she knew, Nathaniel might be lying in a ditch, gassed, or shot and in an unmarked grave. She was overtired and overwrought. She would go to bed early and take comfort in her children in the morning.

As Pretoria lay in her lonely bed, she determined to spend as much time with Susannah as she could, in order to get to know her, and for the child to become confident in her company. If her marriage was to be devoid of emotion, she would ensure that was not the case with her children. She would love them without smothering them and teach them to love in return.

So it was that Pretoria spent the next few days taking both the children out for walks while the weather was fine, playing with them on the nursery floor and encouraging Susannah to take part in the care of Arthur. At bath time, the little girl took pleasure in passing Pretoria the necessary sponge, soap, or towels. Sometimes she held the feeding bottle and liked to stroke the baby's face with one finger. Once or twice, she asked for Grandma but proved easy to distract.

As Elise remarked, "She gives no trouble, but is merely exhausting to be with, for she has boundless energy and an alert mind which leads to constant chattering and a thousand questions."

One afternoon, Pretoria took her to Sylvie's Emporium in town and ordered several new dresses and pinafores, so that the much-darned articles could be thrown away. Susannah was thrilled with the whole process and loved to touch the fabric and choose colours. Standing still to be measured was a trial for her, but they got the task done. Afterwards, Pretoria took her to buy an ice in the little shop on the corner, and the lady there made a great fuss of her. Susannah gave the charmingly cheeky smile which Pretoria recognised so well.

"Just look at those blue eyes," the shop lady said. "Like two bright periwinkles, they are."

"What's a pewitinkle?" The little voice piped up, and everyone smiled or laughed.

"Periwinkle," said the lady behind the counter. "It's a beautiful little flower, just like you."

The next day, they were feeding the ponies with grass and a carrot. Pretoria showed Susannah how to hold her hand flat and tuck in her thumb while Arthur slept in his perambulator. They didn't see or hear Nathaniel come up the drive.

CHAPTER 23

Laden with his kit, and in the crush of men in the same position, Nathaniel couldn't wait to get home. The heavy packs on his back, his relatively new steel helmet, and his rifle were second nature to him now after all the months away, but he would still be pleased to lay it all in a corner and forget it for the next ten days. Ten days of normality, clean sheets, good food, and above all else the quiet of the countryside. No whizz-bangs, no shells crumping, and no snap of rifle fire. That constant noise was the most unsettling. With only the cockerels, cows, wild birds, and horses, he would relax, maybe. He wanted to lie in the grass and listen to a bee buzz, or to lay in a proper bed and hear the t'wit and t'woo of a pair of owls.

Above all, he was utterly desperate to cast his eyes on his wife. Oh, how he had missed her, the scent of her hair, the feel of her slim waist … but he mustn't go there. He had promised to leave her alone after she had done her duty. He could still take pleasure in being around her, though.

Gathering outside Ypres, at Poperinge, there was a huge crush of men, all waving their papers. Nathaniel feared he'd never get away, but he did. Coming over on the boat from Boulogne, some chaps were singing, "Ighty iddley ighty, Carry me back to Blighty." It was all tuneless. Their faces were brown and weather-beaten, but so tired. He presumed he must look the same.

Nathaniel had been lucky enough to get a bath in Boulogne and most of the mud had gone, though not quite all. Other chaps were still caked, and he knew that in London they would be seen as heroes. They weren't. They were survivors.

He took a taxi over to Euston from Victoria. It wasn't far and he could have walked easily, but it saved the stares, and he didn't want the noise and dust. He got some views of London, too. It all seemed so strange after such a long time.

There was a woman selling flowers at the exit to the station. She had a huge basket over one arm, and Nathaniel suddenly had an urge to smell the blooms. He approached.

"Here, love, you can have them, no charge. You've done your bit for us. Nearest I could get to red, white, and blue." The woman thrust a bunch of white and purple and red blooms at him. Stunned, Nathaniel mumbled his thanks and turned, burying his face in the soft ruffles of the petals.

Now he stood at the end of his drive, savouring the whole of his leave stretching before him. The best moment. He looked at the house with the sun shining on the red roof tiles and tall Elizabethan chimneys, and no sight was quite so dear, except that of his wife. His breathing became shallow, and his heart rate quickened. His knees were weak, and he put one hand on the gate post for support. How would it be? Trying so hard not to crowd her or do the things he longed to do…

Pretoria returned to the house and took the children up to the nursery, where she kissed each one and handed them over to Elise, who was preparing their luncheon. As she headed back down the stairs, there was a commotion coming from the hall. She could hear Cook's tones and then a deep male voice. She hurried round the bend in the stairs and fairly flew down, leaping the last three steps as she might have done as a child. "Nathaniel!" she cried. "I didn't know you were coming home."

"I didn't know myself," he said and put out both hands to take hers.

Pretoria was vaguely aware of Cook holding some drooping flowers and mopping her eyes with a handkerchief before she turned away. Nathaniel kissed his wife on the cheek. *Still aloof and formal*, she thought.

Then he laughed. "I was sitting in the front line, minding my own business, because all was so quiet, when an orderly came from the office looking for Captain Moore. 'I'm he,' I said. 'You're to go to the Orderly's Office,' he said, and I thought I must have done something wrong. When I got there, the adjutant said, 'Captain Moore, you're going on leave.' Well, I…"

Pretoria could stand the inconsequential small talk no longer. "And now you're here. It's marvellous. How long have you got?" She wanted to pull him closer, but all she did was give his hands a squeeze before letting go.

"Another eight days. I had to take a day with travelling. And I need to save one for my return."

"Eight whole days," she said. She hoped with all her being that things would be easier during that time. As it was, they were constrained, but then it had been almost two years since they had been together. "What would you like first?" Pretoria asked. "Food, a change of clothes, I'm sure. Something else?"

She glimpsed a sparkle in his eyes, but he shut it down with speed. "I'll go and wash the journey away and change out of this old uniform."

"Cook will have it clean and sorted in no time." More mundane conversation. "I have so much to share with you," she said hopefully.

"Perhaps we might go for a walk, or even better, a ride up into the hills."

"That would be lovely." Her voice sounded stiff even to her own ears, and she sighed as she watched him climb the stairs.

She went to organise the saddling of the horses. This was not how she'd imagined their first meeting. Her hair was mussed by the wind from her time outside with the children. Her everyday dress was alright, but not a colour she would have chosen had she known. Still, a ride out would be good. They would have to talk if they were alone and maybe, just maybe he would take her in his arms and… Warmth rode up her back and around her neck. A flush suffused her cheeks with the tingling she experienced lower down.

The ride was marvellous, the weather was perfect, and they could see for miles. They found a sheltered hollow and dismounted.

"Let's sit, and you can tell me all. Then I would like to see the children. Arthur will not even know me." Nathaniel sounded wistful.

I'm not even sure I know you, Pretoria thought. "Where to start?" she said. "There is so much to tell. Tamsin has gone missing." She told him of her frantic dash home.

Nathaniel listened intently. "It does sound as if she has gone to work on the land, which is highly laudable, but it would help to know where, and that they are both well and being housed appropriately."

"Exactly." Pretoria rushed on. "Everything is well with the estate. Peter is still with us, of course. It was good of him to stay on, and he and I decided to go ahead and sow the oats I told you about. They are growing well, even on the higher land where the soil is poorer. The calves have done well and made a good price at the market. We had one that had scours, but we caught it early, and it was treated, successfully, with water therapy. The dam is fine, too. Oh, I'm so pleased you are home. It's good to talk."

"You have done exceedingly well."

"Peter teaches me constantly."

"And now, mignonette, my Preti, tell me of this little girl, Susannah."

Pretoria hesitated with tingling apprehension. Here it was. It could be avoided no longer, but he had called her by his pet name. What did that mean? "You must meet her. She's lively, intelligent and chatters all day," she said brightly. "In truth I could not turn her away. Such a drama we had when the old lady who brought her to me passed away so unexpectedly. She had been ill for a while and only just managed to travel all the way from her hometown to us."

"This you told me in one of your letters. What of the child?"

Pretoria took a deep breath. She was gabbling. She must calm herself if she was to tell the story with conviction. "Maud Lawson, who married a Mr Hatch, and I were the closest of friends when we were children," Pretoria said. In an instant, the words were out before she had time to consider further. "When both she and her husband were killed, the nursemaid, Mrs Harris, brought Susannah to me. I understand it was Maud's wish, if anything happened to her. Neither of them had relatives, you see." Word perfect. Surely he would notice nothing wrong in what she said.

"That *is* amazing, and so fortunate that you were able to comply," Nathaniel said. Was that a trace of dryness in his tone? Pretoria shot a suspicious glance at him, but his expression was enigmatic.

She continued, adding to her tale. "It is so very sad, because just as her mother was an orphan, so is Susannah."

"Indeed, I see that. Are there no legal papers, no Last Will and Testament?"

"Well, no." Only a slight hesitation. "I suppose they remained in India." This was a bright addition, not previously considered. "Lucy Harris, who brought her, only said it was Maud's dearest wish that I take her. The little one is quite destitute, you see. Her parents' tea plantation was not making money and Mrs Harris was a widow and not a wealthy woman at all, although she seemed quite respectable. You can ask Elise, for it was she who fetched the child from Norfolk after the old lady passed away."

"And you had to arrange the funeral for this nursemaid. It must have been a terrible experience."

Now she was on firmer territory as she described what happened to old Lucy Harris, the doctor coming and the funeral. She ended her story with, "She seems a well-mannered child. Mrs Harris had taught her well, and she's full of joy." She looked at Nathaniel again but could not discern his thoughts, so she spoke with a passion that was true, even if all the words were not. "I couldn't let her go to the Foundling Home. That would be too cruel. Where else can she go? She is the child of gentlefolk and should have a similar upbringing. We can give her that if she becomes our ward. We are wealthy enough, surely. I am convinced you will like her. If something were to happen to us, I am certain we would pray our child would be taken in by someone kind and generous who would love him."

"We have relations who would care for him," Nathaniel said, "but you plead the case strongly, mignonette. So, she is Susannah Hatch."

"Yes, although she calls herself Susannah Harris, which I suppose is understandable. She is still young and spent more time with her nursemaid than her parents, I think. She could keep that name. I think it would help her."

"Why so?"

"I say it for Susannah's sake." Pretoria put all the sincerity she could muster into her tone. "Mama and some of her friends will have known Maud and her husband. You know how they love to gossip. Once they all know Susannah is Maud's child, they will tattle all over the town. We shall be questioned by everyone and have no peace. I wouldn't want such idle talk to reach the child before we have a chance to tell her, when she is older, I mean." Pretoria nodded decisively to emphasise her point. "We could always say she is the child of someone you knew abroad, perhaps? Mama would accept that and soon stop her questions."

"I can tell you have been doing much thinking inside that beautiful head, mignonette," Nathaniel said, and his eyes held the tender sparkle that set her heart beating faster.

"Sometimes, Susannah refers to Mrs Harris as Grandma. She is young, I suppose. She believes the old lady had to go away for a while. I have not told her the truth of that," Pretoria said.

"So many stories," Nathaniel said, and Pretoria's heart gave another jolt. "Well, perhaps I better go and meet this charming, joyous little girl." He stood, holding his hand out to help Pretoria to her feet.

How she wished he would take her in his arms instead of acting like a fond older brother. She supposed he must have seen and heard some dreadful things during his time away, and perhaps he would relax over the next few days. She would do her best to charm him back to how he was before this awful war.

Elise held Susannah's hand as she brought her to the morning room, where Pretoria and Nathaniel awaited her, having returned from their ride. "Arthur is still asleep," she said, "but Susannah is eager to say hello."

The little girl was wearing one of the new dresses that Pretoria had arranged for her. It was blue gingham and emphasised her eyes. Pretoria winced internally and wished she was wearing another colour. Susannah smiled and ran to her. "Elise took me for a walk. We saw the baby horse and I stroked it, but the big ones weren't there today."

"So that's why you have rosy cheeks, my poppet. You've been out in the fresh air." Pretoria stroked the curls from Susannah's forehead.

"Yes, and we went to the river, and I saw some fishes."

"Did you?"

"Yes, and there was a lot of them, but we don't stroke fishes." She giggled and looked back at Elise, who shook her head gently and smiled.

"Susannah, this man is Mr Moore. He's my husband and he'd like to meet you. Say 'how do you do?'"

The child looked at Nathaniel with wide eyes and bobbed a curtsey, but said nothing and leaned against Pretoria's knee.

"Susannah, would you like to see my watch?" Nathaniel took it from his pocket and held it towards the little girl.

The child leaned closer to him to see, and he pressed the catch to open the back.

"Look at all the little wheels inside. If you listen carefully, you may hear it chime." He turned the winder and held it out towards her ear. She laughed with delight, moved closer and looked up into his face.

Pretoria watched her beaming smile and then looked across at Nathaniel, but she saw no sign of recognition, puzzlement, or anything else to give her cause to fear.

"You've been out walking with Elise, have you?" he asked. "Did you give the horse any hay or a carrot? They do like those, especially, but we mustn't give them too many. I think when you say the baby one, you mean the small one?" Nathaniel chattered on, clearly putting the child at ease.

"I like horses. I'd like to ride on one," Susannah said.

Pretoria held her breath. Was there going to be another mention of Uncle Simon? None came, and she relaxed again.

"Would you indeed? Maybe the small one would do for you. The others are too big yet." Nathaniel looked across her head and spoke to Elise. "I understand you collected her —" he nodded at the child — "and her house was quite respectable, but poor."

"Yes, that's so." Elise said no more.

"There are no relatives?"

"No, Mr Moore. The neighbour said there were none."

"You are certain?"

"Yes, sir, none that are known."

"Pretoria has her heart set on making the little one our ward. It seems I cannot refuse." He did not look at Pretoria but bent to Susannah. "Would you like to ride that small pony you stroked?"

The child began to hop about in her excitement, and her eyes sparkled. She clapped her hands and said, "Ooh, yes, please."

"Then we must see what can be done." Nathaniel raised his head and looked directly at Pretoria. "An interesting little face. Such vivid blue eyes. Most unusual. Now, are you content, my dear?"

When Elise had taken Susannah back to the nursery, Pretoria said, "Nathaniel, I am so grateful."

"Right, well, when Arthur awakes I should like to make his acquaintance too, but now I must go and find Peter and ask him about the estate. My time is so limited. Tomorrow there are other things I must do as well, and someone I must see."

He kissed her cheek and left the room, leaving her breathing heavily at his scent.

That night she took particular care with her bathing, using rose water and donning her prettiest nightgown. She brushed her hair until it looked luxuriant. She waited in the big bed for hours, but Nathaniel did not come.

CHAPTER 24

By the time Pretoria awoke the next morning, Nathaniel had already gone to see someone. Julia Worthington, perhaps? After a restless night, she forced her natural strength of spirit to surface and looked at herself in the mirror. The first thing needed was to mend her ravaged features. Lack of sleep had not served her purpose of charming Nathaniel at all; she now had shadows under her eyes and her skin was too pale. Elise would be questioning her at this rate.

Pretoria made up her mind to give Nathaniel no opportunity to see that she cared one jot for his aloofness. If he'd gone to visit Julia Worthington this morning, then so be it. She would certainly not own up to crying last night. But it was exceedingly difficult. Was she to spend the rest of her youth, indeed, the whole of her life with a man who could offer her no more than friendly kindness? An empty future stretched before her. She was determined he would never suspect her true feelings unless he revealed his to be the same. For a brief time yesterday, she had begun to hope. Sometimes she thought she saw the old appreciation in his glance, but he had not shown anything other than brotherly courtesy in the end.

Pretoria's resilience lifted her morale. Her husband would be here for another eight days, so all was not lost yet. She would never demean herself by begging for his love, but she would do all that she could to encourage his attentions, so that he had no need to venture elsewhere again before he had to go back to the front. She would laugh and be merry, ensuring she always looked her best in colourful animation.

Elise, ever quick to spot anything troubling her dear girl, asked after her welfare when they met at breakfast. "And I see Mr Nathaniel slept on the floor in the other room," she said, as if the two things were connected.

"On the floor?" Pretoria was puzzled.

"I have heard it said that soldiers find it hard to sleep in a normal bed when they first come home. Knowing he was out today, I popped in to straighten the room, you see. You talk to Peter ... er, Mr Goodwin. He might know what business Mr Moore is about."

Pretoria looked closely at Elise and wondered why the older woman had coloured up a little at the mention of Peter's name, but she could not be diverted from her more immediate thoughts. "I'm sure he will," she said.

But Peter could not say, when she saw him an hour later as he crossed the courtyard to the stables.

"Ee, I've done a day's work already with those two," Elise said, when Pretoria returned upstairs.

"Perhaps we need to think about a governess for Susannah," Pretoria said. "She's quite exhausting in her curious chatter and need for activity. I shall discuss it with Nathaniel when he finally returns." She found it hard to keep the acerbic sting from her tone. Elise gave her a piercing look, so she turned to the children again.

Pretoria whiled away the rest of the morning reading to and playing games with the children. The activity with the bricks and a set of wooden farm animals lasted for a good hour, which was a happy circumstance since the rainclouds had rolled in and the day promised to be disappointingly grey. Pretoria even stayed and had lunch in the nursery rather than sitting alone, yet again, in the dining room. That evening, she lay curled up under a rug in front of a roaring fire despite the time of year and tried to read a novel. Still Nathaniel did not appear. She could not concentrate and dropped the book at her feet.

Finally, she heard hoofbeats on the driveway, and sat up with haste, folded the rug and smoothed her hair. She had already applied perfume and wore the blue dress which she knew suited her well.

It was only a few minutes before Nathaniel arrived. He was still travel-stained, his boots splashed with grit and his hair blown every which way, lending an extra charm to his good looks. At least he had not waited to come and find her. Was this a guilty conscience? Pretoria smiled warmly, welcoming him home and saying, "I've missed you. I hope your day has been satisfying." She did not hope that at all if he had been visiting Julia Worthington.

"Distinctly hard work," Nathaniel said, "but satisfying, yes. Let me go and change and I shall tell you everything."

This was mysterious. Pretoria began to wonder if her suppositions were incorrect, but where on earth had he been all this time?

Nathaniel could not wait to set eyes upon his wife. He'd been apart from her all these hours, and he'd missed her desperately. She could not have accompanied him, however. It would have slowed him and possibly been the cause of failure. Despite his weariness after a long day, involving wild goose chases and false leads at first, he had greeted her briefly before going to put on clean clothes. Now, returning to the drawing room, he took a deep breath outside the door before he entered. Pretoria stood to one side of a roaring fire, the light of which cast a warm glow across her face, down her voluptuous upper body and across her slim hips. He gulped. How could he resist this beautiful woman?

He held out his hands and she took them both in the softness of her own. As he leaned towards her to give her a kiss, she smelled delicious, and it was all he could do to kiss her cheek and leave it at that. She was warm and respectful, but no more, it seemed. He must stick to his part of the bargain if his life was to be bearable and he was to keep her in it. Perhaps once this war was over, they would come together again.

"Come and sit here with me." He indicated the settee. She sat, so close yet so distant. He took a deep breath. "Let me tell you what I have been doing today."

She looked down at her hands in her lap. "Please do, for I'm dying to know." But then she took a deep breath and, when she looked up, her smile was dazzling, and set his heart racing all over again.

He hurried on before other thoughts took over. "I listened to what you said yesterday, about Tamsin and her young friend." Pretoria seemed startled. *Where on earth did she think I was?* He wondered. He shrugged and carried on. "First of all, I ascertained from your father, at the store, that she had not returned, so I called at the address on the leaflet you told me she had taken. It was a sort of house but full of offices. I spoke to a most helpful lady who sat behind a typewriter. I explained about Tamsin's disappearance and her age. I had a letter from your father to verify what I was saying. Anyway, she gave me several addresses of farms who had agreed to employ Land Girls recently."

"I'm stunned. I had no idea that is what you were doing."

"I had the idea, Preti, as soon as you told me, but I didn't want to say at that point. It may have all come to nothing and would, then, have been an even greater concern. I understand how much your sister means to you, so how could I do anything else, mignonette?"

"I hardly dare ask, but did you have some success, then?"

"I did." He gave a cheeky grin. He couldn't resist teasing her a little, for the delightful expression with which he was rewarded.

Pretoria gave a small bounce next to him. "You taunt me. Did you find her?"

"Yes."

"And is she well? Is she safe? How is she living?"

"Steady on, my sweet, and I shall say. She is living, as you might expect, with several other girls, including Gisela, who is also well and safe. They have been sleeping in a sort of dormitory in a barn. There were camp beds, a little rough but out of the wet and the draughts. Tamsin told me about her worries for her friend, and I think I was able to allay her fears. Gisela will not be taken to an internment camp as some men have been. I'm sure she will weather the storm of any abuse, and your father and mother have agreed to protect her, as will the Strong family, I am certain. After all, her mother is sponsored by them as Izzy's tutor. Tamsin has not exactly enjoyed the work, but she has managed. She may be petite, but clearly she is strong in both body and purpose. I spoke with the manager and explained how young they are. He was surprised. In the end, I arranged with him to organise a cart to take them home, where it will be decided by your parents whether they return to the work or not."

"The cost of all that must be great," Pretoria said. "I cannot thank you enough."

Nathaniel shrugged. "It's a small price to pay for your happiness, and that of your parents, of course. I suggest, in a day or two, we take the children and visit your family home, so you may see for yourself that all is well, and you may hear what agreement has been reached."

Pretoria clasped her hands together beneath her chin, raised her shoulders in excitement and beamed at him. "That would be perfect," she said.

"And now I must go to the kitchen and steal some food from Cook's cupboards, or I may starve to death rather than a bullet finding me." He laughed, although Pretoria did not.

CHAPTER 25

As they trundled along together, looking, to anyone who might observe them, like any happy family, Pretoria couldn't help but smile. The grass gently steamed with the return of the sun and the birds were singing and enjoying the freshness of the day, too. Her husband had also returned, her truest love, and he sat beside her, humming tunelessly to himself. Every now and again he looked at her with those grey eyes that sent her soul soaring. No one would guess of any underlying tensions between them. The children were snug, lying in the back of the cart surrounded by rugs.

She reflected on all that he had done to trace her sister, because he knew how fond she was of Tamsin. He had spent a whole day of his precious leave on an errand to put her mind at rest. He cared for her, most definitely. Not in the way she wished, though. However, they were on their way to her parents' home. She loved Nathaniel more than she had ever loved another, and she would cure this reticence of his, somehow. If only she could be certain he held no lingering fondness for Julia Worthington. She might bring the wretched woman's name up in conversation and judge his reaction. She spent the next few minutes thinking how to phrase it.

Just then, Susannah piped up from behind. "Are we nearly there? I'm very hungry."

"Not so far now, little one," Nathaniel said, looking over his shoulder and smiling at her.

Susannah returned his grin, only more so. She was beginning to show signs of hero worship, and Pretoria could not have been more pleased.

"Look at that big bird over there," Susannah said and pointed her stubby finger at the bird in question. It sat upon an ancient fallen tree trunk. "Its's so big. Is it a vulture?"

"A vulture? Where in heaven's name did you hear of those?" Nathaniel laughed.

"In Elise's book about a place called, um … Am … something."

"America?"

"Yes, America."

"No, it's not a vulture." Nathaniel smiled at Pretoria before turning his head again. "It's a red kite. Look at its colour. The shape of its tail is like a triangle when it flies." He momentarily passed the reins to Pretoria while he made a triangle shape with his thumbs and forefingers. "A shape like this."

"A red kite," Susannah repeated, and then turned the words into a tuneless song as she chanted them over and over.

"I think we may need to engage a governess for this one," Nathaniel said.

"I was going to speak to you about that. Elise mentioned it, and I told her I would discuss it with you, but I didn't want to ask you for yet more. You have been so good about my family and this little one already."

"If we're taking her on, we'll do so properly," he said, brooking no argument.

"Elise will be pleased. I think she finds the two children together quite tiring."

When they reached Pretoria's family home, they were greeted warmly by Marie. "I hope you are not *trop fatiguée*," she said to the family in general, after they had embraced.

Pretoria and Nathaniel shared a quick conspiratorial glance at each other. Some things never changed.

"Ah, I see my grandson has fallen asleep. He might lie on the settee and continue his slumbers. Much better for him to awake naturally. And this is little Susannah?"

"Yes, the daughter of someone Nathaniel met while abroad." Pretoria jumped in quickly with her explanation. She had repeated the story several times already in her head, and was becoming less guilty at each telling. However, each time Nathaniel was involved, she burned with shame, still.

"You all look divine," her mother said. "I see living in the country agrees with you. Susannah's a vital little thing, is she not? What lovely eyes. They remind me of someone, but I cannot think of whom, for the moment. Come, come. I shall organise refreshment after you have been to your rooms and freshened yourselves from the journey. Sally will show you upstairs." She clapped her hands imperiously and a young girl arrived. She must have been waiting on the other side of the door, for she arrived speedily, and Pretoria decided the redoubtable Sally must be used to her mistress's orders.

Once in the drawing room, after reassurances of Michael's slowly improving health in the sanatorium and conversation revolving around general matters, Tamsin joined them.

Pretoria leapt to her feet and embraced her sister. Nathaniel kissed her on each cheek and Tamsin looked suitably chastened. Susannah curtseyed prettily and smiled shyly at the newcomer.

"Why, you must be Susannah," Tamsin said. "Such a pretty little girl. Why you have eyes just like…" She stopped and looked at Pretoria before hastily finishing, "Just like a forget-me-not."

"A forget-me-not," Susannah said, looking up at Pretoria. "What's one of those?"

"It's a pretty blue flower, poppet."

Susannah smiled and sat down close to Pretoria, while she peeped around the room at the new people she did not know.

"So, where is Gisela? I must say you look no worse for your adventure, though you have considerably more colour in your face. You look like a country girl, sure enough," Pretoria said.

"Gisela is back where she belongs," Marie interrupted. "With her mother."

The novelty of being back at home with my parents will be wearing off fairly soon, Pretoria thought.

"I do think that Tamsin's motives were highly honourable," Nathaniel said.

"Well, yes, I do see that." Marie was begrudging, but Nathaniel knew how to manage his mother-in-law, and Pretoria was appreciative of it. He was a truly remarkable man.

Clearly, Tamsin was grateful, too. She beamed at him and then gave Pretoria a surreptitious wink while her mother wasn't watching. "The country needs forty thousand of us girls of the Land Army, and so far there aren't even half of that number. You will know that food shortages are increasing after last year's bad weather and with all the men away. Look what I got." Tamsin dug in her pocket and pulled out a khaki circlet of fabric. "It's got the red crown on it, look. It's my official armband."

"Tamsin, honestly," Marie said.

"It's a darned site better than working in a munitions factory and getting yellow skin from the TNT they work with. You wouldn't want me being a Canary Girl."

Nathaniel nodded. "The chemicals they work with are quite toxic, Mrs Redfern. Tamsin is much better off working on the land. Perhaps she could do, say, three days each week. You would know where she was, and she's absolutely right. Working in a factory would not be a good option for her."

"I shall discuss it further with Tamsin's father later this evening when he returns from the store."

"Oh, of course. Forgive me. I don't mean to influence your decision," and the expression on his face was so earnest that even Pretoria was almost taken in by it.

Once Mr Redfern came home, the conversation turned to other events from the last few months. "Fancy the royal family changing their name in July," Marie said. "How confusing. Imagine if we suddenly became Mr and Mrs Bluetree or something strange." She laughed a little raucously.

"It really was no longer appropriate to be Saxe-Coburg and Gotha," Mr Redfern said, "and Windsor is very regal."

"Like the castle, I suppose," his wife added. "They could have chosen Stuart or anything."

"I suppose some other things were considered, but as a dynasty name, it seems fine," Nathaniel said.

That night, Pretoria and Nathaniel had to share a room. Her mother assumed all was well, but Nathaniel said he would join her shortly and she should go up without him. Her anticipation was palpable. She had checked and rechecked her hair and adjusted the neckline of her nightdress, ensuring an amount of cleavage showed. She tingled all over, and there was a fluttery empty feeling in her stomach as she sat propped against the pillows. As time slipped by, her eyes became heavy, but she managed to stay awake as her ears strained for sounds on the stairs.

Despite her determination, she must have nodded off, because she only became aware of Nathaniel's presence when he climbed into bed beside her.

"It's very late," he whispered. "I took a stroll around the garden and didn't realise the time. Go back to sleep, my dear." He kissed her cheek and rolled over with his back to her.

She lay in the dark for a long time, willing the tears to stay away.

It wasn't until they were on their way home again that Pretoria had the opportunity to bring up her rival. "While you were away, I heard that Julia Worthington is no longer with Lord Doddington," she said.

"I heard as much, on some gossip grapevine. It no longer has anything to do with me and frankly, I have no interest in any of it."

"You haven't seen her, then, since she left … everyone?"

"No."

The single syllable brooked no further discussion. It was patently untrue, if Margaret Parks was to be believed. She had told Pretoria that Nathaniel had met the woman during his previous leave, and although that was many, many months ago, how would he have forgotten?

CHAPTER 26

As they drove back up the driveway after their sojourn at the Redferns', Pretoria looked at the old farmhouse and said, "It was lovely to see Mother, Father, and especially Tamsin, but I'm pleased to be home."

"You called this 'home'. I'm happy you see it as such. It means so much to me. I have many happy memories of this place and when I am away, as I must be in a day or two, the memories will carry me. You are part of that now." He smiled at her with such warmth, it gladdened her sore heart, like the tiniest drop of water on a parched flower.

As they pulled up, Elise was standing with Peter in front of the house. Nathaniel jumped down. Pretoria waited while he lifted Susannah down and came to collect Arthur from her arms. She had time to observe Peter as he bade farewell to Elise, and she was surprised to see a smile lighten the nursemaid's countenance as a flush crept across her face.

Once they were reinstated in the family home, the need for a governess was becoming more evident and pressing. Elise was snowed under and Pretoria would have the estate work to do when Nathaniel's leave entitlement was done, as well as running the household. She approached her husband about it again, when she knew his mind would necessarily be turned to his journey and his future. She already sensed a tenseness creeping around him as the last two days arrived.

"Are you able to undertake that task on your own? That's a foolish thing to ask. Of course you are," Nathaniel said. "What I meant was, I'm sorry I can't be here to help you choose someone."

"I know, and I'm sorry, too." Pretoria couldn't let him know how sorry, so she turned away before he could see the miserable look in her eyes. She didn't want him to take images of her desolation away with him.

This whole time he had been home, they had been the best of friends, sharing laughter and pleasure in being together, but he had not made love to her. She sensed he was holding so much back, but she had been unable to break through and was left guessing where the root cause lay.

Last evening he had been out, but she didn't know where. She'd wondered if he had ridden into town to visit a certain lady, but she couldn't bring herself to ask him directly. She had enquired if he'd had a pleasant evening, but all he'd said was that he had taken a ride onto the moors for the last time until he could come home again. Certainly, it had still been light when he'd left, and the stars and a nearly full moon were enough for such an outing. Was that true? She could hardly go to the stables in the dead of night and see how hot the horse was.

They drafted the advertisement for a governess together and Pretoria undertook to get it posted in Manchester, as well as more locally. They agreed they wanted someone quiet and efficient but kindly. Her main tasks would be working with Susannah, but perhaps occasionally she would take Arthur too, if their activities took them outside. This would give Elise some relief.

The time came for Nathaniel to go. He had said farewell to the children, and now they were helping Cook in the kitchen while Pretoria and he said their goodbyes. He enfolded her in his arms, and she clung to him. "I shall miss you," she said.

"And I, you. Surely this wretched war will be over soon. The United States forces are fresh, well-armed and making a difference. The Italian army have suffered heavy losses, though, at the Alpine Front. I heard that thousands were killed in avalanches alone."

Pretoria could see and hear that she had lost him already. His mind was back where he had been before, and he was thinking of what was to come. She dreaded it all. For those at home, it was a different kind of stress. The wondering was relentless. The food shortages and the making-do were ruthless. The world seemed grey. She fought back tears and pasted on a smile.

"It will be interesting to see what happens now these Bolsheviks, with Lenin, have taken over in Russia. There is talk of them making peace with Germany. It's not over yet, my sweet. We must battle on."

She clung just a little tighter.

"I must go," Nathaniel said and gently took her shoulders to peel her from him. She watched him disappear around the bend in the drive. After he had gone, she stood forlornly until Elise guided her indoors.

"What's all this about then, lass?" Elise had sat her down in the morning room.

"All what? What do you mean?" Pretoria looked at her.

"Come, on, now. He's not himself, and you certainly are not as you were before he went away that first time. You were becoming closer as a married couple. I thought you loved each other then, and were going to be alright together, after everything."

"It's not surprising, is it? Not after what he must have seen and had to do, since then."

"I could always read you like an open book. You cannot hoodwink me," Elise said. "Is it to do with the child?"

"What do you mean?"

"Now, come along. Were you unable to fool him, as you have tried to with me? I've not said anything all these weeks. Now it's time to have the truth out in the open."

"How did you know? She does not resemble Simon." There was no point in trying to prevaricate. She hung her head.

"Except for her eyes. But it was not even that. Your own manner told me something was amiss. I knew you were trying to hide something. Then, when I saw Susannah, something reminded me of someone."

Overwhelmed by shame and sorrow, Pretoria said nothing.

"When I found the child with Lucy Harris's neighbour, I asked her to describe the young man who came to visit sometimes. She told me of his height, the heavy blond hair that always fell forwards, and of course, the eyes. It was Mr Rashbrooke to a T."

"I see."

When Pretoria finally looked up, the older woman looked at her with eyes that were both kind and sad. "Are you still fretting for him?"

"What? For Simon? No!"

"That lad could have charmed a rabbit from its hole, but he had no care how he hurt you."

"Poor Simon. I am sad that he was killed, but he was a chancer and a gambler with his own life as well as with others. He was a desperately unhappy person under all that charm and easy-going façade. Susannah is his gift to me, and in his last letter, he told me of his sorrow for what he had done and asked me to care for the child."

"Can't you forget that boy now that you are married to a real man, and you are the mother of *his* baby?"

"Elise, you have it all wrong. I love Nathaniel to distraction. It took me a while to realise it, but it's the truth. I think he must regret marrying me, though." She wrung her hands.

"I don't believe that for one moment. Has Mr Moore guessed the truth of the child, then?"

"I don't think so." Pretoria paused and then sighed. "I wonder if he would like to take up with Julia Worthington again, now that she is free."

"Never. Not in a million years. I have seen the way he watches as you move around the room. He looks at you as if he is frightened you will disappear. He loves you, my child. He adores you with all that he has. Of that I am convinced."

"He … he likes me, I am sure, but since the birth of Arthur, he has been cool. He wanted a suitable mistress for this house, and … and an heir. That was part of the bargain, and I needed to forget Simon, and to get away from all the gossip and Mama's continual chatter, I suppose. So, you see, his coolness can have nothing to do with Susannah. It stems from before the time that she arrived."

"I see," Elise said.

"Nathaniel and I have agreed to protect Susannah from idle gossip about her parentage. She will be known as Susannah Harris, and he continues to believe she is the daughter of my deceased schoolfriend. Please, Elise, let us keep this between us."

"Very well."

"I do not wish you to have to tell lies on my behalf. If there are any questions, please direct those to me. I have hated deceiving you, of all people, and I am utterly disgusted at not telling Nathaniel the truth when I love him so much."

"Then we shall share the guilt, for 'tis my belief that when a child is sorely in need, she must have that help, and perhaps without too much scruple as to the means by which it is provided."

"My dear Elise." Pretoria was overcome with love. "How could I manage without you? I have worried greatly about what to do for the best, knowing that the child desperately needed a home. Frankly, it's been exhausting. If anything were to happen to Nathaniel now, I'm not sure how I would manage my guilt at deceiving him."

"God willing, he will return again soon, and in good health," Elise said.

CHAPTER 27

"Have you many people to interview for the post of governess?" Elise was folding the children's clothes after ironing, while Susannah sat at the table with some paints and Arthur was busy banging the bricks together. Pretoria tried to show him how to put one upon another to make a little tower, but he wasn't interested. He seemed to prefer to wave his hand about in a random way, and if the bricks tumbled, he was happy. She smiled at his pleasure.

"I have whittled it down to three. I should be so happy if you would sit with me while I talk to each one. I know what to ask, but I should welcome your opinion, Elise."

"I should be happy to do that. I'd like to know who is going to help here with our girl. What do you know of them already?"

"Miss Pettigrew is young. I should prefer her if she is suitable. I might find her less daunting than an older person. She is a village girl, so she will like the countryside. Then there is a Mrs Boothby. She is an older lady whose husband has died. The third is a Miss Carlin. She's thirty-three and has been a governess to two children in Cumberland. I'm afraid she may prove better than the younger girl; I think she'll know considerably more than I. I should not want anybody fierce or domineering."

"Cumberland. That's supposed to be a beautiful county, but quite wild, I hear," Elise said.

"It's not so far. I imagine she will have somehow seen our Manchester advertisement."

"Perhaps she is well travelled, then. She may have a wider view of things than a young village girl."

"Yes, indeed. We shall have to wait and see." Pretoria stood and lifted Arthur to give him a kiss. "Time for your snack, children," she said. "Let's tidy away a little."

"Do you like my painting?" Susannah held it up and the paint dribbled down the paper.

"Keep it flat and I'll come to have a look," Pretoria said. "Why, it's lovely. I do like the big yellow sun."

"I drew a horse. It's brown, like the one Papa Nathaniel rides."

Pretoria gasped at the words, and tears came unbidden.

The children were in the nursery and Cook watched over them while Pretoria and Elise met the three prospective governesses. Elise had left a tin of Cook's biscuits and some of the brand-new Kia-Ora orange juice drink mixed with cold water in a jug. Cook was happy with that. She had read that the name meant 'be healthy'.

Before Nathaniel had left, he'd said, "Susannah is obviously an intelligent child with a lively curiosity. I've never approved of the view that girls should receive a limited education. You know that. In Susannah's case, for example, it may well be that once she is grown, she'll wish to leave us, earn a living and be wholly independent. Times are changing and will continue to do so after this war is finished. Look at Tamsin, eager to work. Delphi Strong has gone overseas, and Rose works in Manchester now. So many jobs are being done by women and girls. I have every confidence that you will find the right person for both of our children. Do write to me and let me know how it all goes."

His reference to both the children as 'ours' had warmed her heart.

Now, both she and Elise sat in the morning room. Pretoria was fidgety and nervous. She had never had to interview anyone before. She had written out the questions and shared them with Elise. They had decided that as the mistress of the house, Pretoria should ask while Elise listened to the answers and made notes. Afterwards, they could discuss their views and make a shared decision.

Miss Marjorie Pettigrew finally arrived after Pretoria had sat watching the clock creep past the two o'clock appointment.

Pretoria disliked her on sight but tried hard not to show it. She had to give the girl a fair chance, so she smiled and said, "Thank you for coming. Tell me, why would you like this position?"

"Well, I wanted to 'elp out my mother and father; 'e's on the sick, you see. Money's tight."

"I see. What schooling did you have yourself?"

"Normal, I suppose. I like to play with the little 'uns, though." Miss Pettigrew said she had left school at twelve and had helped out at home since then.

"What age are you now, my dear?"

At this, the girl sat up straighter, gave a sniff and said, "I'm seventeen. But I've 'elped to look after little 'uns before."

Her clothes were poor, with well-worn boots that were dusty and down at heel. Upon further questioning, her cultural knowledge was revealed to be limited. Pretoria did not wish to hurt her feelings, so she offered to reimburse her for her journey and thanked her for her time.

"'Ave I got it, do you think? Only I need a job, y' see."

Pretoria didn't want to give her false hope. "I'm sorry. On this occasion you've been unsuccessful, but I do wish you well for the future."

Elise showed the young girl out and when she returned, she raised her eyebrows. "I think that outcome was a forgone conclusion without any further discussion."

"I know. I'm sorry. I couldn't see it working out well. I should have consulted you, but…"

"No need, Preti, love. You are more than capable of making the right decision."

"We have Miss Carlin next; the one who has worked in Cumberland. She sounds dauntingly good. I certainly need you for this one."

At that moment, the front door bell sounded.

Pretoria was absurdly nervous as she stood to shake Miss Eleanor Carlin's hand. The lady greeted her with a gentle smile and with composed, quiet expectation. After removing her French blue coat, she smoothed the skirt of her sober, dark dress, the collar and cuffs of which were pristinely white. Her little hat was not ostentatious but matched her coat. Her hair was centre-parted, mid-brown, and drawn back in smooth wings to a knot at the nape of her neck. It was oddly old-fashioned but neat, and it suited her. Her cool grey eyes took in her surroundings, and when she smiled, her pale complexion shone. She was highly attractive in an unusual way.

"I am seeking a governess for our ward, Susannah Harris. She has come to live with us following the death of both her parents while they were abroad," Pretoria explained.

Miss Carlin's expression grew pained. "What age is she?"

"Four years."

"Oh, poor little one."

"Please, do tell us something of yourself and your experience."

"I believe my letter mentioned my age and that I have been working for a Mrs Henshaw in Cumberland. In Cockermouth. For the last five years. I have a letter here as a character reference." She held it out.

"Thank you." Pretoria took the letter. It was in a sealed envelope, and it was plain the seal had not been tampered with.

"Mr Henshaw is a member of the local council and highly respected in that district. Sadly for me, the children are now old enough to go away to school, and so I must seek another position."

"And before that? If I may ask?" Pretoria said.

"Before that my father died when I was quite young, but he believed I should receive a good classical education and that was as important for a daughter as it would have been had he had a son."

"My husband agrees with that philosophy," Pretoria said. "He is, naturally, away in Belgium."

"I worked for an elderly lady as her companion when my mother also died. I was only twenty then."

Pretoria opened the letter and read that Miss Eleanor Carlin was honest and conscientious. It reiterated what the lady herself had said about working there for five years and that the boys were to attend a boarding school. It also said Miss Carlin was quiet, capable, kindly, and was much liked by the boys for whom she had cared.

"Are you returning to Cumberland? It's a long way."

"I shall stay overnight in Manchester."

"We spend all our time here in the country, the children and I. Would you find that restrictive?"

"Children? You have more than one? I understood this position is for the little girl of whom you have told me."

"Well, we have a baby boy too, but Elise, here, cares for him. Only Susannah would be your responsibility. She has an enquiring mind and is lively. She would need discipline, but it must be kindly. I will not have her physically chastised." Pretoria looked closely at the prospective governess to see if there were any hints of disapproval.

Miss Carlin merely said, in her full-toned attractive voice, "I am entirely in agreement with you. A good teacher should be able to inculcate self-discipline without the aid of violence. I should be happy here in the countryside. I was country-bred, in … the west of England."

Pretoria glanced at Elise. This all seemed too good to be true. It looked as if she might have found a treasure, and Miss Carlin was not at all daunting.

At that moment, the doorbell sounded for the third time.

"Might it be possible to meet the little one?" Miss Carlin enquired.

"I have one more person to meet. Would you be happy to wait in the drawing room? Then I could accompany you to the nursery. I won't keep you long."

"That will be fine. I have my book with me."

"Elise will show you."

Elise returned with the final candidate, the widow. Mrs Boothby was a rotund little lady who said she wouldn't take off her coat. She sat with her arms folded across her chest and didn't smile much.

"Mrs Boothby. Thank you so much for coming." Pretoria started as she had before, trying to sound efficient but friendly.

"Live in, is it?" Mrs Boothby got straight to her particular point of interest, it seemed. When Pretoria confirmed this, she added, "Ah, that won't do for me, then."

"Oh, well, perhaps we could come to some agreeable arrangement if we both felt you were the perfect person for the job."

"And how old is the child?"

"She's four."

"She behaves herself, I hope. Only I don't hold with nonsense, you see. It doesn't serve a healthy, happy mind to give in to nonsense. I've brought up several children, so I know my methods work."

"Quite."

The interview was short, and before long Mrs Boothby was leaving.

Pretoria looked at Elise and blew out her cheeks. "She scared me, never mind a four-year-old." She laughed.

"Me, too," Elise said.

"Shall we show Miss Eleanor Carlin up to the nursery?"

CHAPTER 28

As they opened the nursery door, Arthur was awake in the playpen, waving a silver bell rattle. Susannah was sitting at the table, struggling to thread glass prisms on a stiffened string. The task seemed beyond her capacity, and it was evident to all that she was rapidly becoming red-faced with frustration. A shaft of sunlight made the pear-shaped pieces of glass glow ruby, emerald, gold, and peacock blue. Cook was giving advice to the girl, but it didn't seem to be helping, and relief showed on the woman's face as the three entered.

"They were stretched across the window, but the old thread broke," Elise explained as Pretoria introduced Eleanor Carlin to Cook.

"Thank you so much for helping the children," Pretoria said to Cook. "May we have a tray of tea up here, please?"

Cook stood. "Now that, I can do." She smiled, nodded, and bade the newcomer good afternoon, before taking her leave.

"I thought it might amuse her to try and put them on another string, but it seems too hard for her. I shall have to do the re-stringing myself," Elise said. "They look pretty hung up in the light, though. They should please this little lad." She picked Arthur up and handed him to Pretoria. "Susannah will be hankering to go out and feed the horses next."

Miss Carlin went to stand by the child. "Shall I help you, Susannah? Look, if you hold the thread this way, it will be easier." The prospective governess glanced at Pretoria with a raised eyebrow, seeking permission. Pretoria nodded, and Miss Carlin bent over the little girl, her hand guiding the small impatient fingers. Together, they soon completed the task.

Miss Carlin hung up the string. Arthur, catching the coloured sparkle, uttered a loud, throaty chuckle, which startled them and set them all laughing. The small incident relieved a slight atmosphere of constraint.

As they stood chatting, Pretoria noted how Miss Carlin behaved towards Elise with exactly the right measure of courteous respect for an older person, but her glance kept straying to Susannah's sturdy little figure jigging about at the window. Pleased to see that the woman was watching the little girl so closely, Pretoria decided she must be the right person for the job.

Thus it was, before the tray of tea had arrived, Pretoria had made up her mind to engage Eleanor Carlin, but she raised an enquiring eyebrow at Elise. Elise's smiling nod confirmed her decision.

Downstairs once more, as Eleanor picked up her coat, Pretoria said quickly, "I think my husband would expect me to write to the Henshaws at Cockermouth."

"Of course, Mrs Moore."

"However, I am entirely satisfied." Pretoria thought that had a dignified ring. "If I offer you the post, Miss Carlin, how soon can you come?"

In the act of straightening herself, the woman paused, and a little colour crept over her pale skin. "I … er … *are* you offering me the post, Mrs Moore?"

"Subject to confirmation of your reference, yes. Elise has enough to do. She is my personal companion as well as looking after Arthur."

"There is no reason why I should not start at once." Eleanor paused, then added, "Today, if you wish."

"Today?" Pretoria was astonished.

"I own very few possessions, and I have them with me in a small cabin trunk which I left in Manchester. If I had not obtained this post, I intended seeking one there."

"We can have your things forwarded here without too much trouble," Pretoria said.

"Naturally, if you prefer that I should begin in several days' time, so that you might enquire of Mrs Henshaw…?"

"No, no. If you can remain here now, why not? I think it's a splendid idea." Writing to the Henshaws could wait. After all, she had the written reference already. "There is a small room to one side of the nursery. It's not grand but comfortable enough, I think. If you are content with that, I shall ask for it to be prepared straight away."

"I'm sure it will do very well, Mrs Moore."

"You will need a classroom too," Pretoria said, her mood lightening. "Susannah cannot be expected to learn if distracted by Arthur. However, that can wait. I'm sure you will find enough occupation in getting to know her and winning her confidence.."

Despite her success, Pretoria was not entirely happy when she sat down that evening to write a letter to Nathaniel. The small worm of guilt still wriggled inside her head.

Dearest Nathaniel, It is with great relief that I am able to say I have found a suitable governess for Susannah. Her name is Miss Eleanor Carlin, and she comes with a good reference. When Elise and I observed her with the child, she was sensible and efficient. She has a good background and displays a lot of knowledge. From the answers she gave, I am sure she will be firm but kind. I think she will be a treasure.

Pretoria sat and gazed at nothing as her thoughts overtook her. Susannah had hardly mentioned 'Grandma' in recent weeks and never talked of the children she had known before. Fortunately, 'Uncle Simon' had not been spoken of either. Pretoria and Elise never referred to the deception, and if Elise ever had a guilty pang, she did not show it.

Whenever Pretoria considered Nathaniel's generosity to her and the child, her chest grew tight. She dropped her pen, making a splash of ink on the paper, and collapsed forwards as if in pain. She loved her husband beyond all else. If he survived, she would tell him everything and throw herself upon his mercy. *Please, God, save him, and I will do anything to heal this deep gash that I have created*, she thought.

She blotted the splash and picked up her pen. She couldn't write these thoughts when he was in peril so far away. She had to be cheerful and positive and give him nothing extra to fret about.

Arthur grows and develops so quickly. You will see his smile when you return. Today, he gave such a full-throated chuckle, it made us all laugh. Susannah loves to go to the stables or across to the field and feed the horses.

Elise spoke to Peter, and he has been able to sort out a saddle for the little pony. Susannah will have her first lesson in the next few days. She is fearless around the horses, as she is with everything else.

Again, Pretoria's thoughts roamed. Of course the little girl was fearless around horses. Hadn't Mrs Lucy Harris said that Simon had been able to ride anything he was set on, from a young age? Susannah was her father's child in this respect, although none would know this except for herself. She sighed.

We shall need to convert one of the rooms to a schoolroom, so that Susannah might learn without the distraction of Arthur's noises. I wondered about the box room at the other end of the house on the same floor as the nursery suite. It is close by and would not take much work. I am happy to do the clearing and cleaning. Perhaps I might engage someone to do the painting and someone to fabricate a little desk. It is light enough with the gable end window, and the view is not too distracting. For example, it does not overlook the fields and the horses. I should like to make the curtains. Do write soon and tell me what you think.

Peter and I continue to meet regularly, and he is drawing up a sheet of finances to share with you. Everything seems in good order, so you have no need to worry on that score.

In the meantime, I remain the wife who loves you and as you see, I am being dutiful in my care of everything.

Pretoria

She sealed the letter and wrote his service number, name, rank, battalion and regiment, so it might find him wherever he was. Then she propped it on the desk, ready for posting tomorrow.

Over the next few days, she found that the more she saw of Eleanor Carlin, the more she liked her, and she soon decided that here was someone with whom she could become friends. Although the governess behaved towards her with the respect due to the lady of the house, there was nothing subservient about her, nor did Pretoria wish there to be. She was well-read, better so than Pretoria, and she possessed a quiet sense of humour. Pretoria often walked out with her when she took Susannah and found her calm reserve to be soothing.

She and Elise seemed to get on well, too. "She is a sensible woman with no fuss, and Susannah seems to like her very much, which is a good sign," Elise said when asked.

Pretoria was pleased that everything in the nursery quarters seemed to be moving forwards without friction.

CHAPTER 29

"I've had a letter from Mr Nathaniel," Peter said. Pretoria sat in his little sitting room, ready to look at the most recent financial sheets he had produced. She was adept at understanding them, now, and often was able to make a suggestion for improved production. Peter didn't usually share the information the two men exchanged. Pretoria assumed it would be a repetition of the things Peter had discussed with her.

"All is well, I hope," she said. "His last letter to me spoke of what's been happening since Soviet Russia is asking for peace with Germany."

"He's well, my dear. Do not fret on that score. Hard to say who were the losers out of that peace treaty. The Russians are being asked to yield swingeing amounts of pre-war territories to Germany and over half of her industries."

"I suppose with all the unrest in Russia after this man Lenin has seized power, they had no alternative, and now it sounds like all-out civil war there. No one seems to know exactly what is happening, and as for their royal family…"

"It's a worrying thing. They are cousins to our own royals, too. Surely the rabble wouldn't dare hurt them. Exile, maybe," Peter said.

"But not here, it seems. The king won't extend his hospitality that far."

"Rumours are rife, my dear. Yes, I heard, at my club, that King George has been desperate to keep Russia in the fight as an ally and so doesn't want to upset the new regime. My friends were saying that since the Tzar has all his money in our

British banks, the king, who everyone knows is cash poor, wants to keep it that way. The money would eventually come to him, should anything happen to the Tzar."

"That sounds awful," Pretoria said. "I understand we wouldn't want Soviet sentiment here, against our own royal family, but that doesn't seem right or proper at all. What of those four girls and the little prince, Alexei, who is so poorly?"

"I think they're all prisoners somewhere, so we shall see. Now, this letter…"

"Oh, yes, I'm sorry. What does Nathaniel say?"

"He tells me about his time back in France. Actually, he seems more positive than he has been for a while. The German spring offensive has been bad, of course, but not as devastating as it looked at one time. All that trouble over winning Passchendaele, and still the enemy took it back. It must have been so depressing for all our boys." Peter shook his head. "It looked serious for a while, but our combined forces were just too much for them. Anyway, you probably know that. The thing is, apart from all that, he asks me to look favourably on a Captain Phillips, who should be visiting us soon. The man brings a letter of recommendation with him. Apparently he lost his thumb and two fingers, but they patched him up and sent him back. Then he lost a leg, poor blighter. He's been in hospital for months, over there and then back here. It seems that Mr Nathaniel has known him for all that time and would like to help him. Work will be scarce when all our boys finally come home, especially for someone who is disabled, as this fellow is. "

"Oh, poor man. How is he faring now?"

"I gather they've fitted him up with an artificial job. Our Nathaniel thinks he might be an assistant for me here. If it hadn't been for this blasted war, as you know, I'd have retired long ago."

"I know, Peter, and don't think we are not entirely in your debt. I certainly am, for I'd have been completely lost without you."

Peter shrugged. "Oh, ho! It's been my pleasure to work with you, ma'am." He looked embarrassed. "I couldn't possibly have left you … and Miss Elise, ahem, pardon me, on your own."

Miss Elise, Pretoria thought. *I suppose she seems so to him, at his age, although there is only about fifteen years between them. Not so many more than myself and Nathaniel.*

"When might we expect this Captain Phillips?"

Peter perused the letter in his hand. "Could be any day, I think. Nathaniel says he has a first-rate brain and is keen to learn more of management. He was brought up on an estate north of here and has some experience from working alongside his father before the war."

"We shall wait and see, then. If Nathaniel recommends him, I'm sure he will be of help to you."

"Indeed, Miss Pretoria, ma'am."

She smiled. He never knew how to address her, despite her saying he could just use her given name. She had grown to love this blustering old man with his kindly smile and encouraging voice. "Now, shall we move on and look at the finances?"

Two days later, Cook came to find Pretoria in the nursery. "There's a man come to see you." She puffed and tapped her chest. "My, it's a long way up here. Phew."

"A man?" Pretoria asked. "Did he give a name?"

"Sorry, yes. Captain Phillips, he said." Then she added in a whisper, "I think he's got a peg leg and his hand's been all shot up, by the look of it."

Pretoria jumped up off the floor, where she had been playing with Arthur. She patted her hair, brushed down her skirt and descended the stairs to the ground floor to meet the man.

He was not tall and had an open, kind face. A moustache half-covered a wide and generous mouth below a long straight nose and high forehead, which he touched with the two fingers he had remaining on his right hand. "Mrs Moore, I'm right pleased to meet you. Mr Moore spoke so much about you, I believe I already know you. He showed me your picture, too. So proud, he is. I hope all is well. Sorry, I'm talking too much. Always do. Bit nervous, you see, ma'am."

"No need to be nervous at all, Captain," Pretoria said. "We have been expecting you. My husband wrote."

They were about to go through to the morning room when Eleanor and Susannah came in through the front door. The child beamed at Pretoria. "Look what we found." She brought her hand from behind her back and held out a bunch of wildflowers, including campion, vetch, buttercups, and oxeye daisies, all with drooping heads.

Eleanor looked at the newcomer and nodded, before saying to Pretoria, "We're going to find some water for them and use them for some counting work. Each flower has a different number of petals."

"Yes, and after we're going to paint pictures of them, aren't we?" Susannah looked up at Eleanor, who evidently shared her happiness.

"That's marvellous," Pretoria said. "Just before you go, this is Captain Phillips."

"Hello," Susannah said, and she looked pointedly at the man's right hand.

He bent down on one knee, so they were eye to eye. "Hello," he said. "I'm pleased to meet you. You have a sunny smile like one of your buttercups there."

Susannah grinned at him. "Everyone says I'm like a flower."

Captain Phillips looked up at Eleanor from his position on one knee and said, "Pleased to meet you." He stood up again with some difficulty.

The governess took her charge by the hand. "And I, you."

The captain's eyes followed her as she swayed towards the stairs.

"Shall we go to the morning room? I'll ask Cook for some tea, and perhaps we might introduce ourselves properly." Once seated, Pretoria said, "I can't call you Captain Phillips all the time. My name is Pretoria."

"I know that, ma'am. Your husband often spoke of you, as I said. Men over there are not often so open about their emotions, but he missed you, ma'am. Of that, I'm certain."

Warmth wrapped itself around her heart and she smiled.

"It's an unusual name, but it's grand and it suits you," the captain said.

"My father was feeling patriotic after activities in the Cape Colonies, but now I'm stuck with it."

"Aw, our names are just a convenience. It's by what we do, ma'am, that we are remembered."

Pretoria liked this man. "Thank you, and what is your convenience? How shall I address you?"

"I'm Philip. Philip Phillips. Not very imaginative and I don't much like it either, but I shall hope to be of service, if you will take me on."

They chatted and finished their tea. Philip was warm, funny and self-deprecating in the stories he told, helping Pretoria to feel less fearful of what Nathaniel might be experiencing. "Let's go and meet Peter," she said. "Peter Goodwin is the estate manager. He's a marvellously kind man and has kept this place going in the absence of my husband." She explained how he wanted to retire but had specifically stayed on to be of assistance. "He should be back at his cottage by now."

CHAPTER 30

The weather was another player in the unfolding scenes on the Continent. All through May and into June 1918, the sun caused the dust to rise like smoke from under the feet of the soldiers in France, ensuring the German army were able to forward their plans. They were determined to launch a massive make or break assault. On the 9th and 10th of that month, however, heavy rains caused mud and destruction, when German soldiers were bogged in liquid-filled swamps or drowned in watery shell holes, and artillery could not be moved or replenished with ammunition.

The Allies used all the meteorological skill they had acquired and benefitted from that of the Americans. They were able plan their own countermoves, ensuring aeroplanes were deployed accordingly for observation, and using cloud positions to hide their approach for bombing raids, which was a newer and more successful strategy. Ground troops were better prepared to attack through fog banks when least expected by the enemy, but sometimes fate played a part, too.

On the 10th of June the wind changed direction and tens of thousands of gas shells, fired by the Germans, did more damage to their own lines than to the Allies, as the deadly fumes were blown back to them. Decisive action was out of the question when their own troops were muzzled for hours with masks. Officers were unable to give cohesive orders and the men were forced onto their own limited resources.

It was also difficult for Nathaniel and his Company to bear the weather, yet again, but this time they were defending rather than trying to push forwards. The offense on the Marne region to the east of Paris, by the enemy, was recognised as a failure and little seeds of hope began to germinate all around Nathaniel.

Two months later, Peter, Philip, Eleanor, Pretoria, and Elise were sitting on the terrace outside the morning room in the warm August sunshine. Arthur was taking a nap. Susannah was picking daisies, which Pretoria and Eleanor were gradually threading to make long chains. They wound them around the little girl's hair and neck.

The men were quietly speaking of the usual topic. Philip said, "I read that General Ludendorff referred to the defeat by the Allies as the 'Black Day of the German Army'."

"Please God, this is the beginning of the end," Elise said and looked at Peter for confirmation.

"I think it may well be, lass, and it won't be a day too soon."

They were all easy in each other's company, and although Peter still preferred his own cottage in the evenings and sometimes invited Elise to eat with him, the other four frequently took dinner together in the dining room of the big house. Pretoria had encouraged this over the last few months. She welcomed the company and enjoyed their conversation. Social and political barriers were being broken everywhere, it seemed, at home as well as on the Continent.

In September the Hindenburg Line was broken and in the Middle East, Australians began to win the day at Damascus. Pretoria read in the *Manchester Guardian* that the German Kaiser had received a deputation from his High Command to inform him that the war was as good as lost. His navy had mutinied at Kiel, after being forced back by the Allies and in October, the Turks surrendered.

When the Armistice was declared in November 1918, Pretoria could not imagine what it must be like to be in France with Nathaniel, and to hear the guns' silence. How could she comprehend what he had heard, seen, and smelled for nearly four years? She was almost frightened of his return.

Finally, a letter from Nathaniel arrived. It was short.

Dearest Pretoria,

I cannot tell you how I am, for I do not know. I have all my body parts, I have my mind, but it is all so quiet here, and it is confusing, to say the least. It could easily descend into disarray and a madhouse mess, with so many of us desperate to return home, and I'm frightened for that.

There is a ray of optimism. I may be among the primary departures, as they are sending miners and agricultural workers home first. Pray that this is so. I cannot endure much more, now that I know it is over, although almost everybody wants the same thing, and some must wait longer.

Pretoria shared this letter with her friends around the table that night when all five were, unusually, together.

"I have written to the Ministry," Peter said the next day. "I've told them we need Nathaniel here, as he runs a large agricultural establishment."

In gratitude, before she had time to think, Pretoria flung her arms around the old man.

He turned to Philip, who stood quietly at his side. "We'll have to have an Armistice more often."

All three of them laughed, and Pretoria kissed Philip roundly on each cheek.

"What was that for?" he asked. "I haven't done anything."

"Oh, but you have. You did your bit over there at great cost and you're here now, helping us all."

Eleanor stood by and watched with a gentle smile.

The first that Pretoria knew for certain that Nathaniel was back in England was when she received a card, pre-printed in red ink that simply said, *I've arrived in England. I have to go to Canterbury for ten days for demobilisation.*

The waiting was almost unendurable. She passed much of the time in the nursery with the children, since the weather was too cold to be outside.

Trumpets could have been blowing, flags should have been out. Every member of staff on the estate could have been on the front steps with the family, ready to greet Nathaniel with riotous applause. However, Pretoria sensed that he would need quiet and understanding to meld back into his old life. She must be the strong one, here. She had done her best to describe the children's little milestones in her letters, but it could not possibly be the same as living with them.

She had been watching from the window for hours. The inactivity made her nervous, but she would not leave her post.

Then he was there. Pretoria flung open the door and watched him walk up the long drive. She wanted to fly to him, but all she could do was stand and wait, because her legs would not have carried her.

Nathaniel saw his wife standing with one hand on the doorframe, as if she needed support. The darkness of the room behind emphasised the vibrancy of her shining hair, and her peacock-blue dress showed him the curves of her fine figure. Nathaniel dropped his bags and stood like stone as he took a deep, deep breath. Then he closed the distance between them, with each stride covering more than a yard, so that in seconds he was with her. For that moment, all was forgotten as he wrapped his arms around her slim frame and breathed in the perfume of her hair, her body. He was aware of her arms, tight around him, and her hands on his back. His shoulders relaxed and he revelled in the warmth of her.

He pulled his head back to look at her, taking in every tiny feature. The flecks in her blue eyes sparkled; his fingers itched with the desire to cradle the soft curves of her cheeks. Her lips were full and pink and lightly moist, imploring him to place his own upon them. He leant down and kissed her gently.

Oh, how he wanted to sweep her into his arms and carry her upstairs, lay her on their bed and gently undo those prim buttons, but he must not. He had promised, all those years ago, to leave her alone after she had done her duty. He hauled his lips from hers and hugged her again, positive she would feel his racing heart.

CHAPTER 31

Life remained informal as they all tried to resume routines. It was only six weeks since the Armistice had been signed, and there was euphoria, but it was tainted by unease that it was an armistice and not a peace treaty. This would be the fastest way to end the misery and carnage, they said. Perhaps a treaty would follow in the new year. No one could bear the thought of a resumption of hostilities now. Surely the Germans must feel the same, since it was they who'd requested the armistice and it had taken several weeks of wrangling to achieve it.

Now, as the end of December approached, the household prepared for a Christmas like no other.

Eleanor and Elise made paper chains with the children up in the nursery. They were using anything they could find, from old newspapers to brown wrapping paper, and a few grocery bags which the adults had cut into strips. The children were to colour patterns on the paper with crayons and paints, before gluing them into interlinked circlets. The women would string them across the ceiling to gladden everyone's spirits. Arthur's scribbles were much praised, and Susannah made genuine attempts to repeat shapes in a pattern. The tip of her tongue poked out as she concentrated on her task.

Nathaniel had gone into town to have his hair cut and on the way back he would bring a Christmas tree. Pretoria had not had a proper tree for years, not since she'd lived with her parents. She was particularly looking forward to decorating the tree and starting some family traditions that would, hopefully, last for years to come. When she'd been young there had always been a woollen toy robin to place near the angel, which sat with pride at the top. She loved the little bird because it reminded her of a story Elise had read to her during childhood, about a brave robin that fetched some tinsel for his wife's new nest.

Once the children were occupied, Pretoria went down to the kitchen to help Cook prepare vegetables. There was a new pot boy, who stood on a stout wooden box at the sink. His name was Joseph, and he was eight years old. He'd replaced his older brother, who was now old enough to work on the farm.

"You're making a good job there, lad, and it'll be extra Christmas cake for you and your family. I'll make up a parcel with a piece for each of you," Cook said as she kept an eye on him while she peeled potatoes.

Joseph turned. His chubby face was rosy from a good scrubbing, and he beamed at Cook with rounded cheeks and crooked teeth.

They were finishing their tasks as Nathaniel reappeared. "That was an interesting experience."

"Oh? You look very smart," Pretoria wiped her hands down her apron. "Why was it interesting?"

"I had to wear a paper mask in the barbers, and he wore one too."

Pretoria shook her head and said, "Ah the pandemic. This dreadful Spanish Flu. It's killed eight thousand in the last month, but for some reason that number seems to have plummeted, thank goodness. No one seems to know why that is, but it couldn't have come at a better time. As if we haven't had enough."

"They were limiting the numbers in the shop, the butcher told me, when he called here the other day," Cook said. "One in when one left, apparently. Maybe those measures are working."

"Lloyd George might have won a landslide victory with his 'country fit for heroes' pledge, but he won't be able to control a natural flu and the lives it's still claiming." Pretoria frowned and shook her head.

"Let's hope that we'll all keep well if we wash our hands a lot, and wear those masks when we're out, like in the posters," Cook said. "Did you hear that, Joseph? Remember to wash your hands." She wagged her finger at him. "Changing the subject, I was lucky to get a turkey. They're really scarce. It was kind of you to give a chicken to each family on the estate, Mr Nathaniel."

"We shall have a rare old feast, judging by the mountains of vegetables you've prepared there. That bird smells delicious. It's all around the courtyard. I'm not sure I can wait until tonight to eat it." He laughed.

"I'm cooking it really slowly today, so it'll be succulent and not too dry, and then tonight it'll be hot with the gravy. I'll do the pork for tomorrow and then both cold on Boxing Day."

"You'll have earned a day off," Pretoria said. "It's going to be marvellous to have such a relaxing festive season. Together." She looked at Nathaniel.

"Now, I must go and get the stable lad to give me a hand with the tree I managed to find. There doesn't seem to be as many of those, either. Not enough men back home to cut them yet, I suppose. When it's standing in a bucket of sand, we can all hang something on the branches to decorate it."

"Yes, and we must each make a wish when we light a candle," Pretoria said. "It's to be a tradition."

The children's paper chains were a motley collection of colours and shapes, but everyone was pleased with their collective efforts. Pretoria, the governess and the nursemaid draped them around the nursery walls and ceiling and secured them with little pieces of water-activated starched paper.

"It must be time to decorate the tree." Pretoria rounded everyone up, and they went downstairs. "Daddy has a box of little ornaments, and candles in holders with clips. Cook has given us some small nets full of nuts and sugar sweets, and I've tied ribbons into bows. Let's go down and have a look in the box and decide what we're going to use."

The next hour was spent draping long threads of beads, and hanging all the other things on the tree. The lower branches were positively drooping from the weight of everything the children hung, and Pretoria decided she would balance it out later. It was so rewarding to see this family tradition being initiated. Nathaniel climbed a wooden ladder and placed the angel on the top with reverent care. When all was done, they stood back in a circle and held hands. Philip winked at Eleanor as he took her fingers in his own and Peter stood next to Elise. They all gave three cheers and raised their hands in glorious unison.

Higher up on the branches, away from the danger of interfering little fingers and the hems of dresses, all their candles awaited. They each made a wish as they lit their own. Nathaniel lifted first Arthur, and then Susannah and guided their lit tapers to the wicks.

When it came to Pretoria's turn, there was only one thing for her to wish. *Please ensure Nathaniel comes to love me as I love him.*

Later, when the children were in their nightclothes and knelt in front of the hearth to send their notes up the chimney to Father Christmas, Susannah asked, "What happens if it doesn't go up? It'll fall and get burned up."

"We better hope it goes the right way, then. Here, I'll help you." Nathaniel knelt beside her and guided her hand as she threw the small scrap of paper with the crooked, immature writing above the flames, and sure enough the up-draught of hot air carried it safely up and away. He did the same for Arthur as the small boy sat upon his knees before the fire.

All the rituals of Christmas Eve complete, it was time for bed, so Elise and Eleanor took the children upstairs after Pretoria and Nathaniel had each kissed and hugged them.

"I think I'll take a turn in the garden before Philip and Peter arrive for dinner," Nathaniel said.

Pretoria watched him go. Then she heard the front door close and decided to find her coat and join him. She saw him standing, as if deep in thought, by the sparse flower beds. Moonlight slanted across his shoulders. Pretoria approached and slipped her hand into his, although she feared rejection.

Nathaniel turned and looked down at her. "Oh, Preti, it's so good to be home. I don't think I shall ever find any place so beautiful. When the guns stopped, I realised I could hear water dripping from the bare branches of a bush. It was so strange. Almost unbelievable. When the announcement came that morning, there was no throwing of hats and cheering. It took hours for reality to sink in."

Pretoria could not allow the present situation to continue. If it meant living apart, then so be it. Nothing could be worse than this constant indecision and wondering about what had gone wrong. She took his hand and raised it to her lips.

"My mignonette," he said, "what have you done to me?"

"I don't know what's happened," she said. "We were beginning to reach an understanding of each other. Nathaniel, what went wrong between us?" Pretoria took a deep breath for courage. "Why are you so distant?"

"When I asked you to marry me, I said I should like an heir."

"And we have little Arthur. He is healthy and strong, but since his birth…"

"Yes. His birth. I was crass in the way I asked for your hand, telling you my reasons, when I knew you loved another. I was so proud of you and the way you held your head high, bravely showing the world your courage."

"Nathaniel, I…"

"Let me finish, Preti. Even if you cannot return the feeling, I truly adore you. I have for years. When Rashbrooke left like that, I could waste no more time. Some other good-looking fellow might have claimed you. So, I took a gamble. I'm not a gambling man but I took the risk, for you. We struck our bargain. Pretoria, I know you do not care for me as I love you. You loved him first and best." He took her other hand and gazed down at her. "We were friends in our marriage, though. But, after Arthur was born…"

"I do love you. Nathaniel, I love you to distraction, above all else. You have been so aloof. I could not get near you. I made excuses. It was your experiences abroad, you had met Julia again, and…"

"Julia! Never that. Do you not remember what you said to me the night our son was born?"

"I have only the haziest recollection of seeing you at my bedside."

"You said you had done your duty and given me an heir. When I asked you to marry me in that stupidly arrogant fashion, I told you if you did your duty, I should leave you alone thereafter. I have fulfilled that promise and it has been at the greatest cost, I can tell you."

"Nathaniel!" Pretoria was shocked. "If I said such a thing, it would have been meant in fun. I have been so miserable, wondering what went wrong. Mrs Parks told me she had seen you with Julia and that you were getting along famously."

"Such a nasty woman. She delights in spreading false rumour. I thought you were still pining for Simon Rashbrooke." He laughed joyously and kissed her. "My darling, what a fool I've been. I love you so much."

"I have come to love you, Nathaniel, more than you will ever know."

They turned to look at the house. "Dinner will be waiting," he said, "when all I want is to take you to our bedroom."

The candles from the tree glowed in the dark. Little wishes and promises of a brighter future.

All through dinner, they kept glancing at each other, and when their eyes met it was with anticipation of the night to come.

CHAPTER 32

While marital relations were resumed and all seemed well on the surface, Pretoria was aware that Nathaniel still did not know the truth of Susannah's parentage. She spent many hours agonising over whether to tell him. Things between them were better than they had ever been. She could not bear to risk destroying that.

Life went on. Nathaniel met Philip and Peter to discuss what was happening with the estate, although, fortunately, the autumn and winter plantings were complete. Pretoria knew that together she, Peter as the estate manager, and Philip had maintained the tenant properties well and the cattle herds were flourishing. She was welcomed at their meetings but sensed her work in this area was done. She wasn't resentful. It was good for Nathaniel's well-being to retake the reins, but she realised she must carve herself a different life.

Eleanor and Philip continued to be invited to join Pretoria and Nathaniel in the evenings for dinner. Pretoria's anxiety over Susannah was eased by the presence of others. She was also pleased to see that Eleanor and Philip enjoyed each other's company, and were growing closer.

Pretoria and Nathaniel began to receive invitations. Pretoria generally enjoyed being part of a wider circle again. It was assumed by all their friends that they were an idyllically happy family unit. Nathaniel was polite at all times, and he regularly kissed her and told her he loved her.

Then, one day when Pretoria had gone into town on the motor omnibus to purchase some ribbons for Susannah and a new toy for Arthur, she met the odious Mrs Parks with her mama in the street. It was the first time she had been there for many months, although Nathaniel often came for business.

"My dear, you look positively blooming," Mrs Parks said.

"Your papa and I would like to come and see you at your house soon," Mrs Redfern said. "We'd love to meet Nathaniel again and to see the children."

" I'm sure Nathaniel would love to talk with Papa again. It's been such a long time."

"And what of this other child?" Margaret Parks enquired. "Do we understand that you and Nathaniel are actually contemplating adopting someone else's daughter?"

"I cannot talk of our affairs in the street," Pretoria said with chilly speed.

Glancing across at her friend, her mother added, "We were dumbfounded. Why do such a thing when you have a child of your own, and are perfectly capable of parenting several more?"

"Mama, please!" Pretoria was scarlet-faced.

"It does seem an extraordinary thing to do, my dear. You are very brave. After all, you may never know what you are getting." Margaret Parks could not resist airing her view. "I trust your husband is well, still. He seemed so, when I last saw him, but I had not the opportunity to speak as he was deep in conversation. I cannot say with whom."

Pretoria wondered how it was that this nasty woman had seen Nathaniel and in what circumstances. Was it true, or did she simply enjoy spreading rumours? Could she not say because she didn't know, or was she simply enjoying making Pretoria uncomfortable? Or had she seen Nathaniel speaking with Julia Worthington? Pretoria trusted her husband, and he had assured her he thought nothing of his ex-fiancée. She believed him.

There was an awkward lull in the conversation.

"We will speak of the child later, when we visit," Marie said. "We thought perhaps Friday afternoon. Would that be convenient?"

"Certainly. I must hurry now. I have what I came for and am expected back at home." With that, Pretoria turned and left the two ladies.

She had already given her parents the agreed version of Susannah's history, but she knew that her mama would hardly let it rest at that. She foresaw a difficult hour or two on Friday afternoon, and she was not wrong.

As soon as Mr and Mrs Redfern arrived with Tamsin, Marie renewed her attack, somewhat surprisingly directing her attention to her son-in-law.

"Nathaniel, what is all this about this child you are taking as your ward? When Pretoria told us about her, we were never so astonished in our lives."

"Risky thing to do, eh?" Mr Redfern gravely stroked his whiskers. "I don't know that I would care to risk it myself. Someone else's child, what! Tricky, tricky, it could be."

"I see little risk attached," Nathaniel said mildly. "We know Susannah's parentage, and she is a bright little thing. Very alert. We have grown fond of her already, have we not, Pretoria?"

"Oh … yes indeed, Nathaniel."

"Parents were friends of yours, I gather. No relations living, eh?" Mr Redfern said. "Very sad."

"None. Elise knew the child's nursemaid and vouched for her respectability. I understand Pretoria has already described what happened to her."

"Died at your home. Shocking business, what!" Mr Redfern said. "Still, I'm sure you know what you are doing." His tone revealed clearly that he did not think so. "I suppose if Elise knew the people too, then … well, she is shrewd. We always trusted her judgement, did we not, my dear?" He looked at his wife.

Pretoria was aware that her cheeks were beginning to burn and turned to her sister. "What have you been doing, Tamsin?"

"Not much," Tamsin said. "Not since I finished my work on the land. I miss it. It was hard, but we all got along well and had some good laughs."

Her mother tutted. "It ruined your complexion, and your nails were *quelle horreur*!"

Tamsin giggled and earned a frown from her mother. "Gisela is back with her mother and Izzy is learning that language again."

Pretoria changed the subject. "What a relief that Michael is mending so well. It's a shame he could not accompany you for this visit." She was determined to steer the discussion away from anything dangerous.

"Your brother has great plans for the school he would like to open, too, so he's very busy with that at the moment." These things were discussed for a while, but inevitably the conversation reverted. "When are we going to be permitted to see our grandson and … and the other child?" Marie asked.

"I shall ask Elise to bring them here." Pretoria stood.

The grandparents gloated over Arthur, who didn't cry at all, and were reluctantly impressed by Susannah, who behaved with customary open friendliness.

She has inherited her father's ability to charm, Pretoria thought with a touch of wryness.

Eleanor soon came to take Susannah upstairs again, but she left Arthur on his grandma's knee.

"What a pleasant person," Marie said as the governess was leaving the room. "She is clearly a lady who has fallen on difficult times." She turned to Nathaniel. "So, Susannah's parents were killed in an accident abroad?"

"A carriage crash," Nathaniel said. "Somewhere in Eastern Europe, we understand."

Pretoria gazed at him with astonishment. She had not thought he would ever lie so blatantly, even to save them from her mother's inquisitive ways. She began to relax and sat back against the cushion.

Marie clicked her tongue. "Dear me, it is really so sad. Exactly like poor Maud Hatch and her husband out in India. Do you remember, Pretoria? I'm sure you were told of it. They left a child, too. A little boy. I heard, only the other day, that he was being cared for by some distant relation."

Pretoria's heart gave a sickening lurch. This was what she had dreaded. She risked a glance across the room and met her husband's eyes. Nathaniel's expression was as hard and dark as flint.

CHAPTER 33

The rest of her parents' visit passed like a sick dream for Pretoria. Somehow, she forced herself to pour tea and listen with apparent interest to Mama's tales of events at the store, and to Nathaniel's explanation of his employment of Captain Philip Phillips. After that one blood-freezing look, Nathaniel had avoided her eyes. Pretoria was ill with shame and fear. There would be no hiding anything now. She would even be forced to implicate Elise.

When Nathaniel went outside with Mr and Mrs Redfern to show them the garden, Pretoria and her sister had a few minutes alone.

"Whatever is the matter?" Tamsin asked at once. "You look unwell. Do you feel faint?"

"No, I … I'm a little tired, that's all. We've had several late evenings, recently." *Here I am still telling fibs, even to my sister*, Pretoria thought with more shame. She had to force down rising panic, for the Redferns stayed late.

"We have booked rooms, so we may stay longer," Marie said. "It's such a long time since we saw you."

"You could have stayed here," Nathaniel said, but Pretoria was exceedingly relieved that they would be leaving for the night.

When it became evident that Marie had no intention of moving until she had witnessed Susannah and Arthur being bathed and put to bed, Nathaniel invited them to remain for the evening meal. Fortunately, Pretoria had foreseen this much, and had requested extra vegetables to be prepared to go with the roast leg of lamb, and a second apple charlotte had been made. There was plenty for everyone, but Eleanor and Philip tactfully refused an invitation to join them at the table, saying that it was the first evening the family had spent together for some time. Eleanor would enjoy sharing supper with Philip in the kitchen. Elise had gone to see Peter again.

Halfway through the meal, Pretoria went to the kitchen to retrieve more custard, using the excuse to escape for a few minutes. She found Eleanor and Philip laughing heartily. To see them both so happy in each other's company would normally gladden her heart, but now nothing could ease her fear.

Retribution could not be avoided forever. At eight o'clock, the Redferns took their leave. Nathaniel and Pretoria stood on the steps under a sky of frost-polished stars, waving them goodbye before they turned back indoors.

Nathaniel said curtly, "Come into the drawing room, please. I think we have certain matters to discuss."

Pretoria preceded him, with her head down and a knot of sick tension gathering in her stomach. He went straight to the small table against the wall and poured himself a glass of port, but did not offer her one. She sat on the edge of the settee, her hands clenched in her lap.

Nathaniel came to the hearth and threw another log on the fire, then slowly straightened to face her. "Well? What have you to tell me?"

Pretoria licked her lips, shifted in her seat, and cleared her throat. Never before had she been so frightened of losing something so precious. Nathaniel's eyes, normally full of light, looked dark, but not with anger. His look was one of infinite sadness, regret and disappointment. This was even harder to bear than shouting. Pretoria tried to speak, but her throat constricted. Tears pricked her eyes.

"Whose child is she?" Nathaniel's said. "You had better tell me, hadn't you?"

"She is…" Pretoria could not speak the words.

"She is Simon Rashbrooke's daughter, is she not? She has those same exceptional eyes."

Pretoria nodded silently.

The muscles in Nathaniel's neck and jaw tightened. "And what is she to you — beyond being *his* child? What … other connection is there?"

It took Pretoria a few seconds to grasp his meaning. Shock loosened her tongue. "What do you…? You cannot think I am the mother. Why, when she was born I didn't even know him then."

A flicker crossed his face. "Yes, yes, of course. A foolish assumption on my part. I've lost track of time."

Indignation made Pretoria sharp in her response. "Precisely. How could you imagine such a thing? I knew him for six months, and you know what occurred. Simon Rashbrooke was found to be a married man. His wife is Susannah's mother. I didn't see him again, after he left back then, and I know nothing of her whereabouts."

"So, she is still alive? This wife of his?"

"I believe so," she said more quietly, "but I honestly don't know where she is."

"We better hope she never comes here, then. So, none of it was true? The orphaned child, totally destitute, no relatives at all? All backed up by Elise. Why? Why did you seek to deceive me so completely, Pretoria?"

"Nathaniel, I don't know how to make you understand. I thought you did not love me, that probably there was another again, and that you married me to gain an heir and to save me from social ruin. You know that I once loved Simon

Rashbrooke and I did not wish to hurt your pride when you had done so much for me. Would you have let me keep her if you had known she is his child? You despised him, distrusted him, and … and that was not all."

"What else?"

"He sent me a letter. He wrote it on the eve of a battle, believing he might be killed, and he was. He wished me to know the truth of certain things, if he died."

"Indeed." The look on Nathaniel's faced showed his scepticism.

"Yes, he wasn't all bad, as everyone thinks. He made a terrible mistake when he was barely eighteen years old. A boy, just a boy, Nathaniel. He became infatuated with a woman older than himself. She was to bear his child. He felt obliged to marry her, but lived to regret doing so, most bitterly."

"How so?"

"She proved to be very possessive. She gave him no peace. They quarrelled and it was often violent. In the end, one day…" Pretoria stopped.

"Well?"

"She stabbed him and wounded him. She is still in prison, as far as I know."

"Good grief. If she ever came here looking for our little girl, I would get the constables onto her, that's for sure," Nathaniel said.

"It was a terrible thing she tried to do, and Simon took the baby and hid her. Lucy Harris was his nursemaid when he was a child, and she looked after Susannah. It was she who brought me Simon's letter."

Nathaniel leaned his elbows on the mantelpiece, his face in his hands. "Oh, my God, what a mess," he whispered.

"You may well blaspheme, for it was a blasphemous thing she did."

"I had no idea," Nathaniel said.

"No one knew and no one must know any of it, for Susannah's sake. Please, you must see that. Simon had his pride. It was almost all he did have." Pretoria hung her head.

"He had your love." The words rang harshly in the quiet room.

Pretoria looked up. "I did love him, yes, although looking back, it seems more like a young girl's romantic notion for a handsome man who tried deliberately to charm her. Simon was at fault in that, I suppose, but I think he loved me in his way. His letter tells me that. And now he is dead and gone forever." She stared at Nathaniel's rigid shoulders.

"And I must compete with that. A ghost. A martyr."

"No! It is no competition. You may read the letter if you wish. It might help you to understand why I wanted to keep Susannah, and why I lied to you. I … I didn't want to lie. Please believe that's true, even if you cannot forgive me." She choked on a sob.

He turned to look at her. "You could not trust me with this secret, but you are prepared to let me read your … your love letter?"

"Yes, if you wish. You are my husband, and I want you to know everything. What I said the other night, about my love for you, is true. I am … bitterly ashamed of deceiving you. I want you to read it." She jumped up. "I'll bring it down." She ran from the room, and he made no attempt to stop her.

As she reached the bottom of the stairs, Eleanor was just disappearing onto the landing above her, but the governess did not stop or speak to her. Pretoria paid little attention as she hurried to her bedroom. She snatched Simon's letter from its hiding place and hurried back downstairs. She thrust the paper towards her husband. "Read it. Please. It's explains the whole thing much better than I can."

Nathaniel looked at it as if it were something corrupt that he did not wish to contaminate him, but then his shoulders slumped. He unfolded the paper and read in silence. Finally, he said, "I see how difficult you must have found it to refuse such a plea." Then he refolded the letter and placed it carefully on the mantelpiece.

Pretoria stayed where she was. Her legs would not have carried her two steps. Her heart was thumping, she was short of breath, but she was beyond tears. She had no idea what would happen next.

"I wish you had trusted me enough to tell me all at the start," Nathaniel said.

"I wish I had. Truly, I do. I should have done. It's just that things between us were so, well, cool, and I was frightened I'd lose you altogether. I didn't know how to tell you, and then you were away, and it didn't seem right to say it all in a letter. You had enough to contend with over there. I couldn't see any child left as she had been, and I decided it would work, somehow."

"We have both been foolish, have we not?" Nathaniel held out his arms, and Pretoria fled to them. "I knew I was taking on a firecracker. I told you I was proud of you, and I am. Against all the odds, we have made a family that is ours."

Pretoria breathed out at last.

"We may have a few problems ahead, however," Nathaniel said against her hair.

She pulled away and looked up at him, but remained in the safe circle of his arms. "What do you mean?"

"Simon had a father, and the child has a mother. She is not the orphan with no relations that I thought her to be. It may take some resolving."

"Oh, but…"

"I know. The grandfather has become a ne'er-do-well, but we must discover more of the mother. Simon stated in his letter that he wishes you to be her guardian, and that is our strongest card, but if the old man is still alive and if the mother is still in prison, he will have a claim. And the mother may even be out of prison by now. We must discover where we stand in these things, and sort it all out properly before it becomes a burden which we cannot alter."

Pretoria looked at him in horror. "But the grandfather is … is a drunkard and violent. Lucy Harris, and Simon, in his letter, have said so. He could not possibly be the right person to have care of her."

"I agree, but it must all be done correctly. We will ensure we keep her here with us, somehow," Nathaniel said. "To be honest, I thought we should pursue things in law, even when I thought she was the daughter of Maud Hatch. My sweet, foolish wife, we cannot take a child without having a firm footing."

"Of course. If Susannah is to be our ward, it must be done correctly. I know that. I've been burying my head all this time."

"We will hope for a happy outcome. As I said before, we do have Simon's letter. I will confess, I always wondered about the child, and your story of the school friend."

"Oh?"

"You are not a convincing liar, my love. Something didn't sit squarely."

"Elise says I'm not good at telling tall stories," Pretoria said.

"Hm, Elise. I shall have to speak with her, too. She has encouraged you in something foolish and possibly dangerous."

"Please don't be angry with her. She advised me to tell you straight away, after she realised. I persuaded her, in her loyalty, to help me."

"I understand that. I shan't be harsh with her."

"Was there anything else that gave away my deception?" Pretoria was still feeling humbled by her husband's kindness.

"Her eyes. At first, I could not recall where I had seen eyes of such a vivid blue. Then when I remembered, my own jealousy confirmed the idea in my mind, and I was consumed with the notion."

"And you said nothing." Pretoria rested her head against him.

"I couldn't bring myself to it, thinking you still cared for her wretch of a father. I was frightened that to voice the thing was to make it real. I couldn't condemn the child, though, and I'd been wrestling with it all, until your mother said the Hatches had had a boy child. I saw your face and it confirmed all my worst suspicions. I knew we had to face the truth and see if there was any hope for our future together."

"I'm so sorry."

"Hush now." He leaned down and kissed her mouth. She tasted the salt of her own tears.

"What should we do now?"

"I shall have to make some enquiries about Susannah's mother."

"Simon came from the West Country. Dorset or Somerset. I think that is where he met his wife."

"That's a good place to start the search, then. I shall make enquiries of marriages, births and deaths, too. Since just after the start of the war, there has been a General Register Office for all of those. Each now has to be certified, so there must be a record of such things, probably in London."

"When will you go to Manchester?"

"As soon as possible, maybe tomorrow. The sooner the better, to get it all sorted out. I have come to love the child as much as you, even in the short time I have known her. I couldn't possibly let her disappear now, without being sure of her well-being."

CHAPTER 34

Nathaniel was gone for three days, during which time Pretoria tried to act as normally as possible. Eleanor was a little off colour, she said, so she took to her bed for a couple of days, and the children played with their mother and Elise or took walks outside in the crisp chill of the short January days.

When Nathaniel returned, Pretoria could hardly wait to hear what he had to say, but she happily accepted his long, hard kiss as he enfolded her in his embrace.

"I have engaged a man to go to Somerset House in London and thence to pursue what he might discover there. He has my permission to travel south if necessary. Apparently it's a vast building with a warren of small rooms, and its staff are beavering away, ensuring this new National Registration is updated and maintained. They are well placed, since they have been responsible for the national census since 1841. Now, where are the two scallywags? I've missed them almost as much as I've missed you. Let's visit the nursery, and then I must take a bath. Perhaps you will help me with that." He gave her a cheeky grin and her stomach swooped.

Their lovemaking was like the blessing of a new beginning. He was gentle, teasing her senses with his lips and his fingers. It didn't take long for her to respond. She regained her confidence and was able to reciprocate his passion as it built. In all the years of their marriage, they had spent so little time together, and were still discovering what stoked the desire of the other. When their final coupling came, it was perfect for them both, and afterwards they lay in the contented euphoria of having acknowledged their love for each other.

They awoke early the next morning. Pretoria lay in a warm blissful haze and turned to watch her husband's sleeping face. The dark stubble on his chin added a rakish attraction to his square jaw that was hard to resist. As he lay asleep, she thought he looked younger, more vulnerable, his dark hair ruffled, his lips drooping like a sensitive boy. *Thank goodness we found each other again before it was too late*, she thought. The experience of last night had ensured they were wholly one again and closer than they had ever been.

She was drifting back to sleep when she became aware of a commotion on the stairs. Pretoria frowned and looked at Nathaniel, who had sat up in a hurry.

"What the…?"

They dressed quickly, emerging to find chaos reigning in the house. Elise had Arthur on her hip and was talking to Cook at the bottom of the stairs. She held her hand to her forehead and looked worried.

Elise turned at the sound on the stairs. "Oh, thank goodness you're here. Have you seen Eleanor or Susannah this morning? I can't seem to find them, and it's early to be out and about. I have a sense that something isn't right."

"We haven't seen them. We've only just got out of bed." Pretoria was embarrassed, fearing their bedtime activities would be guessed at. "Perhaps Susannah awoke early, and they've gone out to look at the horses. It wouldn't be the first time." She endeavoured to be soothing, sensing that Elise was unusually concerned.

"Normally Eleanor wouldn't permit it, until Susannah has done some schoolwork, at least."

"It does seem strange, indeed, but a little soon for everyone to be in a state, surely," Pretoria said.

"I'll go and get fully dressed, in case I need to go further afield." Nathaniel turned towards their own rooms.

Pretoria watched him go. "Further afield?" He didn't respond. She returned her attention to Elise.

"Eleanor has been off colour for several days, and while she was up and about yesterday, she looked very pale and drawn. Not her usual self at all," Elise said.

"Which makes it all the more unlikely they have gone outside, I suppose."

"Exactly."

"I assume you've checked the schoolroom. Have you knocked on her bedroom door?"

"I haven't done that, but I've looked everywhere else indoors."

Pretoria was getting an uncomfortable feeling in the pit of her stomach, but there had to be an explanation. "I'll go to her room," she said.

She hurried up the stairs to the little room in the attic. Her heart seemed to be thumping against her ribs as she arrived at the door. *Probably the climb from the stairs. I'm not as fit as I used to be*, she thought wryly.

Elise was behind her, still with Arthur on her hip. Pretoria pushed open the door and peered around. "Her bed is made, as if she hasn't slept there."

Ashen-faced, Elise passed her and opened the wardrobe doors. "Many of her things are gone. Look, it's half empty. She has been right odd these last few days. What does it all mean?"

"We better check on Susannah's clothes."

Pretoria hurried from the room, her mind in a distraught whirl. An idea had begun to take hold. Eleanor Carlin had seemed so calm, so reassured. Pretoria had liked and trusted her. From where had this idea sprung? Could it be that she was

Simon Rashbrooke's wife and Susannah's mother? She must be the right age.

On reaching the nursery, she flung open the drawers where Susannah's little sets of underclothing lay. Gone. She hurried to the wardrobe. Items missing. The pretty blue gingham dress was gone and one or two others, along with pinafores and a coat. She turned to Elise. "Please will you look after Arthur? I must speak with Nathaniel." Pretoria was in a panic now.

Finding her husband, she told him of her fears. "Why else would a woman take a child, other than for some personal reason?" she demanded. Other spine-chilling possibilities sprang to her mind, and she guessed from Nathaniel's expression that he had similar thoughts. "She seemed so eminently sane and cool." Or was she a superb actress, hiding the devil knew what behind that level-headed exterior? She thrust the idea from her mind. Such unspeakable horror could not be faced. If her original notion was correct… She prayed it was, for if Eleanor was Susannah's mother, the child would not be harmed. Eleanor might be a desperate woman, reckless enough to recover her child, but she surely would not harm her.

"I'll look in the stables and ask Philip. They seem close. I'm sure he'll know if anyone does." Nathaniel hurried out.

Nathaniel's mind and heart were in turmoil as he left Pretoria. He had come to love Susannah, with her fetching smile, sparkling blue eyes, and confident chatter. If Eleanor Carlin was indeed her mother, the situation was complicated. There was no formal process of adoption in Great Britain, and the woman had a mother's rights. However, Nathaniel had been led to believe they were not great with her background of previous imprisonment, and with the letter that Pretoria had thankfully kept from Susannah's father.

He had contacted the new National Children Adoption Association and had spoken with the founder Miss Clara Andrew herself, who had been most encouraging when he'd told her of the circumstances. She had questioned him closely about his and Pretoria's background and current situation. Now that Princess Alice, Countess of Athlone, had become the patron of the Association, they were pressing for greater formality, although the government had stated they could see no need for it. Currently, papers were being processed that would acknowledge Nathaniel as the legal guardian of Susannah. The powers that be had agreed his home was the best place for her. All this flew through his mind as he hurried across the courtyard to the stables.

"Where is the gig?" he demanded of the stable lad, who jumped to attention at the firm tone of his master.

"Miss Eleanor asked for it to be readied yesterday evening. She told me you had said it was alright and that she was visiting her aunt for a couple of days, Mr Nathaniel, sir. Is everything alright, sir? Did I do wrong?"

"No, lad. You're fine." Nathaniel shook his head and rushed outside again. Then he stopped and turned at the door. "Have you seen Mr Phillips this morning?"

"Yes sir. He was going down to the bottom paddock, I think, sir. Said the fence needed a repair."

That's something, at least, Nathaniel thought, *although Eleanor would have been safer with an escort.* On finding the captain, Nathaniel demanded, "Have you seen Eleanor this morning?"

"No. It's a bit too early for her to be out with the little one yet. They don't normally take a walk until after lunch. Is everything alright?"

Nathaniel let out a sigh and shook his head. When he was able to speak again, he said, "Has Eleanor said anything to you of her background?"

Philip looked sheepish. "She swore me to secrecy. I saw no ill in it, since she is an entirely reformed person. The very telling demonstrates that, I think. She was circumspect at first, but finally told me everything."

"Oh? I think you better tell me all, for it seems she has left us."

"My goodness." Philip seemed genuinely shocked. "I had no idea she was planning to go. I thought we were becoming close, since she'd told me about her past. I can't believe it. She's gone? She never said anything about that."

"What did she tell you, Philip? I need to know."

He looked uncomfortable. "She begged me not to say, but I do owe you everything, Nathaniel."

"It will go no further than is absolutely necessary, but I must know." He took a deep breath. "She has taken Susannah."

Philip gasped. "Oh no! I can't see why she would do that. She has everything here that she wants. She told me that." He proceeded to tell everything that Nathaniel already knew. "It seems Simon cheated and lied to her constantly and gambled their money away. She told me of her final disgrace of being imprisoned for what she had done to him. I admit I was shocked at first, but there's no denying she loves that little girl. She did say that while she was incarcerated she had time to think about why Mr Rashbrooke behaved as he did. She came to realise that he was a damaged person, and she has forgiven him. She swore she has learned to control any temper he generated in her and believes that is not her normal state. I must say, Nathaniel, in her defence, I believe what she said about that. She said on more than one occasion that the little girl is well off here, and has many more opportunities than Eleanor could ever hope to provide."

"I suppose sometimes people are thrust into something because of a very particular set of circumstances." Nathaniel sighed again. "Thank you, for your honesty, Philip."

"If you need me to accompany you anywhere to find them, I shall gladly come. I do believe I love her," he said with simplicity. "She must have a reason for fleeing like this, though what that might be, I don't know."

"I might take you up on that offer." Nathaniel took out his pocket watch and glanced at the time. "I'd like to get on the road. Eleanor has several hours on us."

CHAPTER 35

Nathaniel and Philip rode at a trot where the lanes allowed. The hedges were bare of leaves and the cows not yet out in the meadows. It was a bleak journey both in outlook and mission. The first place to stop was the town ten miles away. Eleanor and Susannah would need a change of transport and the horse would need stabling, so that was the obvious place to start looking for them.

"We'll go to the stables at the inn, first. I'm guessing she would have been aiming for Manchester, or even Liverpool. It's easier to lose oneself in a city, and she could be thinking there'd be a greater likelihood of work."

"She could go anywhere if she's off to Manchester. She could catch a train if she gets that far. She hails, originally, from Dorset way. Would she go back there, for the familiarity?"

"I don't know, but she had her most unfortunate time there, so maybe not. The more I think, the worse I feel. She could go anywhere. It's the proverbial needle. We need to catch up with her as soon as possible." Nathaniel had a hollow feeling in the pit of his stomach. He would rather not involve the constables, but it was looking increasingly likely that would be necessary.

"Let's not put our umbrellas up before it rains," Philip said. "We'll see what they say at the stables."

"Yes, you're right." Nathaniel looked across at his companion. "How are you doing, with the leg? If you need to rest, let me know. I know we're in a hurry, but I'd rather you are able to travel. I'm so pleased to have you with me."

"It's fine. I'm used to it these days. It doesn't hold me up much."

They made good time, and after enquiring at the inn stables, they discovered that a lady with a sleepy child, wrapped in a blanket, had taken the coach out that morning heading for Manchester. She hadn't taken a room, having arrived late in the night, but had camped on the bench seats in the parlour. She had left a gig and a horse and asked that it be returned to a Mr Nathaniel Moore, but had paid for the service.

"Well, well, that's me," Nathaniel said. He arranged for the animal to be stabled until his return in a few days, when he would collect it. He also paid for the two horses on which he and Philip had arrived to be cared for, and he hired another to take his own gig onward.

"I don't want to wait until tomorrow for the next coach," he said to Philip. "We might lose the trail."

The next few days were the worst that Pretoria had experienced since Nathaniel had come home from the Continent. It seemed as if over the last few years, she had lurched from one crisis to another, and she was exhausted from it all. She was tempted to call her parents' department store on the new telephone that Nathaniel had fitted only last month, and speak to her father, but she couldn't face her mother calling her back. Mama would be constantly exclaiming and speculating, and in no time at all the news would be all around the town. Susannah, and even Eleanor, must be protected from that. If it became public knowledge that Eleanor had served in prison, all their lives would be intolerable. People would judge them for employing her. They would lose all credibility in their community and Susannah would be judged by the faults of her parents.

When the telephone finally sounded, Pretoria rushed to pick up the handset. Nathaniel's voice crackled on the line.

"Do you remember when I went to the General Register Office? Well, I discovered there that Susannah's mother's name was Elizabeth Caterham."

"I see."

"Philip tells me now that Eleanor is really Elizabeth Eleanor Caterham."

"So, it's conclusive. She is Susannah's mother. I still don't understand why she has taken our little girl away with her."

"Neither do I. Philip said she was happy here and had everything she wanted, with access to her child and a hand in her upbringing."

"God speed, my love. Let's hope for a happy outcome with all this."

They finished the call and hoped that the operator was discreet, since Nathaniel had had to make the call that way. There was no automatic exchange in their area yet.

Pretoria spent the next twenty-four hours chiding herself for accepting the governess's credentials so easily. She had meant to check them, but Eleanor had seemed so eminently suitable that it didn't seem worth it. Now, she assumed that the letter of recommendation must have been written by Eleanor herself, and not by Mrs Henshaw in Cumberland. How could she have been so naïve?

By the time Pretoria heard from Nathaniel again, she was beginning to feel ill with anxiety and lack of sleep. The sound of wheels on the gravel at the front of the house brought both Pretoria and Elise to the door at a run, since Arthur was in bed and asleep.

The gig had pulled up, and Nathaniel was climbing down with Susannah in his arms. As Pretoria rushed down the steps, she could see by the light above the door that the child was pale with dark circles around her eyes.

"She has been overcome with carriage sickness, on and off, for the last few days," Nathaniel explained in a quiet voice. "She's quite unharmed, but she is exhausted from being unwell in the carriage from Manchester. We didn't delay in coming from there, because I knew how worried you would be. And I wanted to be here with you."

Philip climbed down too, and came around the gig to stand beside them. Pretoria put her hand on his arm and reached up to kiss his cheek. "Thank you so much," she said, but she could see how unhappy he was. She could only assume he was disappointed in what had transpired with Eleanor, when they had become close. "Come through to the kitchen, Philip. Cook will find you something. I know she's not abed yet."

"We must get the little one into bed as soon as possible. I'm happy to stay with her." Elise reached out.

As soon as this was settled, Pretoria wanted to know everything. "Where is Eleanor now? Where did you find them? You must be exhausted. I'll ask Cook for a plate of cold food and some soup."

As they sat in the snug and Nathaniel ate his supper, he told Pretoria all that he could. "We found them in a cheap room near the station. It was a rough place, though fairly clean, I suppose. Eleanor was planning to take the train to Liverpool, and from there to seek a berth on a ship bound for America."

Pretoria gasped. "Imagine if that had happened. We would never have seen our little one again." Tears of exhaustion and relief sparkled in her eyes.

"But it didn't happen," Nathaniel said. "She is safe upstairs and will remain with us."

"And where is Eleanor now?" Pretoria asked.

"She travelled back with us and a policeman. We could do nothing else, since we had to seek help in Manchester in order to find her."

"She's not in the common jail with … with … again, is she?"

"No, my dearest. She is lodged in the constable's own house, albeit under lock and key."

"Why did she do it? Why did she take Susannah from us?"

"I am still not sure. Tomorrow I must go back to the town and speak with the police, since she claims to be Susannah's mother. It does sound as if she is, if what she told Philip is true. That must be verified, though."

They were both too tired to make love that night, but took comfort in each other's arms as they listened to the wind playing through the branches outside. Nathaniel stroked Pretoria's back and she kissed his naked chest, marvelling yet again that this man had chosen to love her, and still did despite everything.

As if he could read her thoughts, he said, "I am blessed to have you in my life, Pretoria. If you had said no to that ridiculous proposal in the park, I'm unsure how I would have survived. I have loved you for years."

"Despite all this grief I have caused?"

"You may have acted a little rashly, I suppose, but it was with the best of motives. You have given me a charmed existence. I have my family around me now, and I have you to see me through, with all your bravery and loyalty."

CHAPTER 36

Pretoria and Nathaniel slept late, and after making up for their separation and tiredness the night before, they lay for a further half an hour, luxuriating in their satiation of each other. Then they visited the nursery, where Susannah seemed none the worse for her adventure.

Nathaniel swung Arthur above his head, which made him chuckle in his deep-throated way, before cuddling him. When the little boy complained, he laughed, mussed his hair, and returned him to the floor with his bricks.

"Ah, Mama Preti," Susannah said. "Where is Eleanor? She's a sleepyhead, this morning."

The term of address made Pretoria smile, but then she said, "Eleanor went to see someone. Papa Nathaniel and I will go and see her this morning."

"Can I come?"

"Not this time, poppet, but we shall return at tea time. We should see you before you go to bed at any rate, and you will have fun with Elise."

"Yes, Mr Goodwin said we could ride in his cart and go to see the new calves up at Knutscombe farm," Elise said.

Susannah clapped her hands and hopped from foot to foot.

Nathaniel took control of the situation with apparent ease when they arrived at the constable's house, and Pretoria admired the way he handled the policeman with enough deference to ensure he was helpful, but skilfully manoeuvred him along in the conversation.

"I understand from our conversation yesterday that you have a letter. May I see it, please, sir?" the constable said.

Nathaniel, with Pretoria's prior agreement, passed Simon's letter to the officer. "Certainly, but I should like your assurance it shall remain confidential between us. I wouldn't want this information to become common gossip in the community. I'm sure you understand that. Oh, and I shall require a receipt for it."

"Well, on second thoughts, perhaps you will keep it, sir, on the understanding that should I need to see it again, that will be possible."

"Indeed. Thank you. I shouldn't want my wife to suffer unnecessary upset with idle chatter."

"I should like to see her," Pretoria said.

Both men turned to look at her, considerably startled.

"Well, now, ma'am, that may not be allowed," the constable began awkwardly.

"My dearest, what purpose could it serve?" Nathaniel asked.

Pretoria clasped her hands. "I ... I want to talk with her. The description in Simon Rashbrooke's letter does not fit the Eleanor Carlin *we* know. We both liked her. You thought her intelligent and kind. I believe she has suffered. Clearly she did a bad thing after Susannah was born, but perhaps she has changed, learned her lesson in a very bitter school. I should really like to discover why she ran away with the child when everything seemed to be going well and they were both happy with us."

"Surely it is obvious if the girl is hers," the constable said. "She must have been planning it all along."

"I know it appears so." Pretoria gathered her thoughts. "I have the strangest feeling there is more to it than we think. I *must* talk to her. Please, Nathaniel."

"Ma'am, it wouldn't be regular. If charges are to be brought against this female..."

"I understand, constable," Nathaniel said, "but under the circumstances, surely you could arrange it."

He sighed. "Very well, sir. Please take a seat and I shall speak with her."

When he returned, the constable took them along a narrow passage to the back of the house and unlocked a door. It was a dull day and the small room seemed dim, lit only by the light from one barred and latticed window. There was no fire, and the room was furnished only with a plain scrubbed wooden table, one chair, and truckle bed against the far wall. Eleanor Carlin was sitting on the bed, wrapped in a grey blanket for warmth. She was bent almost double in a foetal position and paid no attention to the noise of the opening door. Pretoria was shocked at the change in her looks. She had always been pale, but now she looked drawn, and ill to the point of total exhaustion. Strands of hair had escaped her neat chignon, and her clothes were creased. She did not move but merely stared at them with dull eyes, accepting their intrusion like one who is beyond caring.

Pretoria approached, standing a yard away from her. The two men stayed in the open doorway, watching. "Eleanor."

There was no response.

"Are they treating you well?" Pretoria asked gently.

A nod. "How is Susannah?" The words came out slowly, as if the speaker's lips could hardly form them.

"She is quite recovered. It was only carriage sickness. She doesn't travel well."

"I didn't know that before." The blank gaze moved, wandering over the opposite wall. "I'm her mother, and I didn't even know that about her."

"You haven't known her long. Not since she was a baby." Pretoria sat down on the bed beside her. "I want to help you if

I can. I need to understand exactly why you took her away."
Looking at the constable, she said, "Can you not leave us alone
for a few minutes?"

"Oh, I couldn't permit it, ma'am," he said.

Pretoria reached over and took one of Eleanor's hands. It
was stiff with cold. "Listen," she said, "I know about you. I
know who you are. You are Elizabeth Eleanor Caterham, and
you married Simon Rashbrooke. They know your history." She
nodded at the two men in the doorway. "Before Simon was
killed, he wrote to me and begged me to take Susannah as my
ward. He told me what you tried to do to him. I think, now,
there was great provocation."

The drawn face turned towards her. "You know I tried to kill
him?"

"Is that how it was?"

"I don't know. I wanted to hurt him because he hurt me, so
many times. I was beside myself with pain and worry. He no
longer wanted me. He was going to leave me and take
Susannah with him."

"You loved him very much?"

"Yes, I loved him." There was an empty desolation in that
one phrase. Then a tiny spark of animation lit her eyes. "I
knew where he would take her. Simon was not so clever. I
knew he would take her to Lucy Harris. She was his nursemaid
when he was a boy."

"How did you find out that Susannah was living with us?"

Eleanor gave a shuddering sigh and seemed to rouse herself,
drawing her hand from Pretoria's. "I shall tell you everything if
you want me to," she said.

"Please do."

"I left prison after I had served three years. I was ill when I
came out." Her voice was toneless. "I knew Lucy came from

that place in Norfolk. Simon probably forgot that he told me that. I got work as a barmaid. I listened and learned. As soon as I could afford it, I travelled there and made enquiries. I soon found where the old lady had been living and that she had a child with her. A neighbour told me that the old woman was dead, and the child had gone to live near here, and she gave me your name."

"Was the neighbour a thin woman with several children?"

"Yes, her husband was not well. I told her I was Susannah's aunt, come back from foreign parts. She was a simple soul and believed it all. Told me several things about where Susannah was and with whom."

"So, then?"

Eleanor gave a weary little sigh. "I decided to make my way to this area and find any work I could, so I would be able to discover where Susannah had come to live and I might see her now and again. Perhaps you will understand this. You are a mother too. It was quite by chance I saw your advertisement for a governess. Pretoria, I beg you to believe this: I meant no harm to your family, and certainly not to Susannah. I only wished to see her, and to reassure myself that she was well and happy. But seeing your advertisement, I seized my chance to be with my child. Fortune was, at last, on my side. I swear, I had no thought of taking her from you." Her head dropped and she lapsed into silence.

"What about your reference letter from Mrs Henshaw? Did you write it?" Pretoria asked.

"No. The Henshaw family are real." Her voice held a trace of bitterness. "Mary Henshaw is my sister. She showed me some pity and wrote the letter to help me, but her husband wouldn't have me near their house."

"I see. What I don't understand is why you ran away with Susannah, after being with us for several months. Why now? Philip told us you liked your position."

At the mention of Philip's name, Eleanor's eyes welled with tears, but she looked up to the ceiling and managed to stop them falling.

"Why now?" Pretoria asked again, ensuring her voice was as gentle as possible.

"Because I heard what you said, or rather what he said." Eleanor looked across at Nathaniel. "You were arguing, the two of you, in the drawing room. I heard my husband's name and stood to listen. I know I shouldn't have done, but it concerned my child. I needed to know. You mentioned my father-in-law. Susannah cannot have anything to do with him. Dreadful man. But then you said you'd get the constable onto me if I ever came near, and I'd already told Philip who I was. I couldn't risk losing my child again. Not a second time."

"Did you not hear the end of the argument?" asked Nathaniel. "We agreed that being with her grandfather would not be in her best interests, but we knew we had to ensure her place with us was safe and secure."

"No, I didn't hear that. When you, Pretoria, left the drawing room, I fled. You may have seen me, but I was at the top of the stairs by then. I was sick with worry. You will remember that I took to my bed for a few days. I knew I had to leave. I was despairing and wretched."

Suddenly, Eleanor was weeping; harsh, dreadful sobs which tore at her whole being. She collapsed onto the bed and pulled the blanket to her stomach, clinging to it as if to life.

Pretoria jumped to her feet and bent over the distraught woman. "Nathaniel, she is exhausted, ill, and freezing cold." Then to the constable, "Surely you can see her distress? This is not an ordinary criminal case. Can your wife not bring a warm drink?"

"Yes, ma'am. I agree this is an unusual case. I'll get her to fetch a warming brick, too."

"Thank you."

They ensured that Eleanor was calm and cared for before they left.

Pretoria said, "We will sort this out. Please do not fear anymore."

CHAPTER 37

There were two days full of enquiries, discussions, news and worry for all of them. Nathaniel was spending hours on the telephone. At the end of the week, a messenger returned from Dorset. Simon Rashbrooke's father was still alive but bedridden from a stroke. There would be no question of him claiming a right to Susannah, even if he wanted to, which he did not. One day she would inherit his estate, being the only surviving relative.

Susannah's mother asked for nothing, imploring only that Nathaniel and Pretoria would agree to keep her child and care for her.

"Surely there is no reason why we cannot continue as we have before," Pretoria said to Nathaniel. "Eleanor must earn her living. We must have a governess, and she has been an excellent teacher. Susannah is already fond of her and has been asking after her whereabouts constantly. I suppose, having lost Lucy Harris, she's frightened of losing someone else. We could share responsibility for the child's upbringing. When she is old enough, I will explain the situation to Susannah. Knowing she is loved and secure will scarcely harm anybody. We are agreed, are we not, that Eleanor is no longer a threat to anyone's safety?"

"I do agree she seems to have been a victim of the circumstances in which she found herself. It seems that since then there have been no causes for concern at all," Nathaniel said. "Do you think Eleanor would accept such a position?"

"I'm certain that she would, from what she has said. She wouldn't be a servant in our household. She hasn't been all this time. She's been a friend."

Two more days passed before Nathaniel was able to secure Eleanor's release, and then he travelled, yet again, to the town to collect her.

Philip stood with Pretoria on the steps as the gig rolled up the driveway. Eleanor sat upright next to Nathaniel, seemingly clinging to any vestige of pride she could muster.

As soon as they drew level, Philip went to help her down, offering his hand. "Look at me, Eleanor," he said.

She turned her head, but her eyes remained downcast. A flush rose up her pale cheeks.

"I'm so pleased you have returned to me," Philip said.

She looked at him as she took in those words, but she still didn't smile.

"When you left, there was a hole in my world. You did what you thought you had to do, but from now on we can discuss what is best for us both."

Tears rolled down her cheeks at the gentleness of his tone. She climbed down and when his arms folded around her slim body, she allowed her head to rest against his shoulder.

"Come. I'll help you to your room and then leave you in peace, but it will only be for a while. I believe a certain young lady wishes to acquire all of your attention."

Eleanor did smile then and allowed Philip to lead her indoors.

Nathaniel put his arm around Pretoria's waist as they climbed the steps to the front door, walked across the hall and mounted the stairs. "I think we have some unsettled business of our own," he said.

"There's something I must tell you, first." Pretoria gave him a dazzling smile.

The following November, on the eleventh of that month, Pretoria presented Nathaniel with another child. Her confinement was significantly easier this time. When he came to see her, she was propped up in their big bed with a new daughter in the crook of one arm. Arthur sat cuddled against her other side and Susannah was perched on the end of the bed, gazing in fascination at this wrinkly pink addition to the family.

Pretoria giggled and gave her husband the widest smile. "Duty done, again, but this is our own armistice."

He laughed. "Another daughter, darling Preti. Now we have two daughters and a son," he said.

"Shall we call her Elizabeth, as we planned? It seems to be a family name now, too, since it is Eleanor's first name."

"By all means, Elizabeth for one of her names, but I think she should be known as that small flower."

"Which is that?"

"The one which is a little wild but has a perfume as sweet as honey and fills the air with its presence. It's one no home should be without. It's called mignonette," Nathaniel said, as he leaned down to gently kiss her.

A NOTE TO THE READER

Dear Reader,

Thank you so much for choosing *The Warring Heart*. If you have also read *Sisters at War* you will notice these two books are connected. I was loathe to leave some characters behind after I had written the last book. As a writer, I become entwined with the lives of my characters. Since publishing *Sisters at War*, readers have asked what happened to some of them, too. That, in particular, influenced the next book in the series, *Resistance of Love*. However, in this one, it's an opportunity to round off some characters, who did have a happy ending before, but as in life, it's always good to catch up with old friends and exchange news.

I have visited Ypres many times and was fortunate enough to attend the ninetieth anniversary of the Armistice there. During the day someone returned the large key to the ancient Cloth Hall that his grandfather had taken during the battle. An elderly gentleman, not hearing properly, asked why he was returning the key to the brothel. This remark was too good not to use in my story, but I used it to create a little levity during a dire situation.

Research took me to the Archives at Kew, copies of *The Wipers Times*, and several personal accounts from soldiers who were on the Ypres Salient. Sometimes less is more and I hope I have given a hint of the destruction of buildings, but also of people, without being too graphic. More, I wanted to maintain the momentum of characters in geographically different places but who have a deep connection. They each need to concentrate on what they have to do but always they have the other at the back of their mind. In real life we do this all the time, although fortunately for most, the circumstances of our lives are not so dramatic. I tried to show, even during those dire historical times, life for those at home was very dissimilar to those in the trenches but also very difficult and often stressful in a different way.

Tyne Cot cemetery near Passchendaele, where 11,961 graves commemorate the loss of life on and near the Ypres salient, is the largest, but only one of many such places. 34,984 names are also inscribed on a memorial there, for soldiers who were missing. The Menin Gate, a tunnel-like edifice at the eastern exit of Ypres, was designed by Sir Reginald Blomfield and is inscribed with a further 54,395 names of unidentified missing soldiers. Hundreds returned home maimed in body and mind. It's an emotional place to visit but I'm so pleased I went. After the traffic has been halted, a silence descends. It is solemn and dignified. The nightly playing of the Last Post by the local fire brigade who honour the dead of all nations, even now, is a simple but moving tribute.

I hope we meet again in the pages of future books involving the Strong and Redfern families.

If you have enjoyed reading *The Warring Heart*, you might consider writing a short review on **Amazon** or **Goodreads**. These, from knowledgeable people, are so important for authors' success but also contribute to other readers' choice of a book. If you would like to know more about my writing, my website is **www.rosrendleauthor.co.uk**. You can also **sign up for my newsletter**. I often give free gifts and there is early access and information about my books. I love to hear from readers, and you are able to connect with me through **Facebook** or via **Twitter**. I hope we'll meet again in the pages of my other novels.

Ros Rendle

Sapere Books is an exciting new publisher of brilliant fiction and popular history.

To find out more about our latest releases and our monthly bargain books visit our website:
saperebooks.com